Advance praise for *I Have the Answer*

"With this surprising collection of stories set mostly in Michigan, Kelly Fordon takes her place among our most compassionate, insightful, and wry observers of contemporary American life. These are stories of mothers and daughters, wives and widows, rendered in prose that is at once poetic and plainspoken, with genuine heart and a connoisseur's eye for the absurd."

—Will Allison, contributing editor at *One Story Magazine*

"Like all bold, transcendent fiction, the stories in *I Have the Answer* end up answering intimate conundrums about love, identity, and relationships with ever more complicated questions. Fordon's characters don't seek to understand their lives so much as find a way to tell a different story about both the past and the future. Vanished husbands are re-imagined as pale images of the men they once were. Teens on the cusp of adulthood grapple with phantom limbs and the true meaning of exorcism and faith. To their skeptics' surprise, 'crazy' characters who claim to have all the answers actually prove they do. Throughout these stories, Fordon's sly humor about middle-class perks—Costco, grocery delivery services, trendy psychotherapy, binge shopping—bind together the women who both rue and rely upon these props. Fordon's deft, lyrical writing and gentle yet pointed comedy create endearing, realistic characters looking for the very answers the reader hopes to find."

—Laura Hulthen Thomas, author of *States of Motion*
(Wayne State University Press, 2017)

"In Fordon's gripping collection of stories about characters on the edge, we witness what happens when life deals a blow—divorce, addiction, empty nests, dementia, death—and they are forced to face the biggest unknown: themselves. In each pitch-perfect story, Fordon takes us to the precipice where trauma and triumph are equal possibilities. The people in these stories are so hauntingly real that long after I put down this book, I found myself wondering what became of them."

—Desiree Cooper, author of *Know the Mother*
(Wayne State University Press, 2016)

"Kelly Fordon's *I Have the Answer* is a remarkable, penetrating, and moving collection that explores what it means to be a good neighbor, a good parent, a good spouse, and a good human being. From New Guinea during the Second World War to suburban Michigan of today, Fordon maps the contours of the heart with an exquisite delicacy and a generosity of spirit entirely unequaled in American fiction. Rare is the author who can bring so much genuine compassion to her characters, despite all of their foibles and flaws, and rarer still the writer who can entertain us immensely as we follow her beloved creations. *I Have the Answer* exudes emotional truths, as certain as they are surprising, on every page."

—Jacob M. Appel, author of *Millard Salter's Last Day*

"In a narrative voice that is stunning and pristine, Kelly Fordon's *I Have the Answer* presents characters who suffer in a self-made darkness of secrets, desires, and longing. While going through the motions of their suburban lives, they are at the mercy of the unraveling of normalcy. In each story, we are reminded that underneath the facade of having it all, nothing is simple or easy."

—Melissa Grunow, author of *I Don't Belong Here*

"Fordon's stories hold up a mirror to our shared humanity, breathing three-dimensional life into her characters through a rotating prism of joy, tragedy, triumph, and heartbreak. This collection joins the ranks of such illustrious contemporary short story writers as Alice Munro, Jeffrey Eugenides, James Salter, and Aimee Bender."

—R. J. Fox, author *Love & Vodka*, *Awaiting Identification*, and *Tales from the Dork Side*

"What a great collection! Again and again, Kelly Fordon's characters charm and disarm us as they face death, divorce, the departure of a maddening child, a diagnosis of dementia, and even molestation. As the world crumbles, they must ask themselves the question, How do I live now? In these big-hearted stories, the answer is to be found in life itself, in living as an act of courage, and living as an art form. Like Lorrie Moore, Fordon proves that comedy is a worthy opponent of tragedy. Times are hard—they're always hard—so read this book and you'll feel better!"

—Bonnie Jo Campbell, author of *Mothers, Tell Your Daughters*

I HAVE THE ANSWER

MADE IN MICHIGAN WRITERS SERIES

GENERAL EDITORS

Michael Delp, Interlochen Center for the Arts

M. L. Liebler, Wayne State University

A complete listing of the books in this series can be found online
at wsupress.wayne.edu

I HAVE THE ANSWER

stories by

kelly fordon

WAYNE STATE UNIVERSITY PRESS
Detroit

ISBN 978-0-8143-4752-2 (paperback)
ISBN 978-0-8143-4753-9 (e-book)

Library of Congress Control Number: 2019954086

Publication of this book was made possible by a generous gift from The Meijer Foundation. This work is supported in part by an award from the Michigan Council for Arts and Cultural Affairs.

Wayne State University Press
Leonard N. Simons Building
4809 Woodward Avenue
Detroit, Michigan 48201-1309

Visit us online at wsupress.wayne.edu

For my father,
Bill Stanton (1924–2002)

CONTENTS

There are more things in heaven and earth . . .

—*Hamlet* (1.5.167–68), Hamlet to Horatio

THE SHOREBIRDS AND THE SHAMAN

Corinne's husband, Ethan, died in his sleep. Right before bed, they'd had one of their rote conversations—the same one they had every night.

"What time should I get up?" Ethan was sitting on his side of the bed with his back to Corinne, fumbling with the alarm clock on his ancient phone. "Should I get up for yoga or sleep in?" He had just retired from thirty years as a high school math teacher and loved the fact that he suddenly had options.

"Blah, blah, blah," Corinne said. "Why do you ask me that every single night as if I actually care when you get up?" Though it sounded awful in the retelling, she'd said this in a playful tone. They chided each other. That was their shtick.

"I've read sleep is as important as exercise. Maybe I should just rest."

"Well, you lucked out, Iron Man. Tomorrow is Thursday. They have spinning not yoga."

"Bonus!" He set the phone down on the nightstand and lay back down. "That's the best news I've heard all week."

Six months later, Corinne could count on one hand the times she'd left the house. She worked remotely as a web designer, so getting dressed was optional. Now she ordered household items from Amazon and food from a local grocery delivery service. She communicated with the shoppers via text and asked them to drop the bags on the front stoop. Days were spent prone on the couch staring at her screen or the ceiling while listening to the Talking Heads' "Once in a Lifetime," the song that had been playing when she'd met Ethan at a fraternity party their freshman year; both anthem and omen, as it turned out.

Their son, Scott, was still in college, and he'd reluctantly returned to school two weeks after the funeral at Corinne's behest. It was tragic to lose one's fifty-five-year-old father, but Corinne couldn't think of a better place to drown one's sorrows than a frat house.

Good one, Ethan would have said.

Corinne had smiled and spoken in complete sentences while Scott was home, and she was still able to muster up a chipper persona every time he returned for the weekend or for a holiday, but she discouraged frequent visits because maintaining the facade made her feel like a windup toy whose key was rusting out. Plus, she had to pretend that she wasn't smoking. Thank God for the upstairs porch off her bedroom.

The most persistent friend—the only one who was still trying to engage on a regular basis—was Anne. Anne was a family therapist who practiced three days a week out of her house. Her husband was high up in his company and had not been seen during daylight for more than a decade. Up until Ethan's death, Anne had always leaned on Corinne. In fact, the last time Corinne had consulted with Anne on any significant issue was back when Scott was a high school sophomore and had claimed that the pot smell emanating from the basement was Taco Bell takeout. Corinne had been horrified by the pot and the lies and had convinced herself that it was only a matter of time before Scott joined the small band of junkies who hung out next to the highway onramp. When she told Anne, Anne had not talked her off the ledge like a good therapist. Instead she had agreed and handed her rehab pamphlets. It had been Ethan, finally, who'd convinced her that she might be overreacting by reminding her that she was high the night he'd met her back in college.

"As I recall, you enjoyed your fair share of Taco Bell," he'd said.

The saddest part about Ethan's *saving saving saving* for retirement was that it hadn't prevented him from dropping dead four months into it. And now there was no financial reason for Corinne to ever leave the house. One morning when she was lying in bed contemplating a mid-morning nap, or, more accurately, embarking on one, Anne called to see whether she was free to spend the weekend at her cottage on Lake Erie. Because Anne's daughter had left for Bates in the fall and her husband remained a phantom figure, Anne was always looking for an escape hatch. She was always onto some new scheme— paleo diets, thirty-day yoga bodies, philosophy seminars, master gardener classes. Her problem was her marriage, but instead of facing it, she was like a woman trapped in a dinghy on the high seas, lighting one sparkler after the next.

In the end, Corinne agreed to the trip because the cottage had been one of her favorite places to visit with Ethan. Plus, it would give her something to tell Scott besides the fact that she had burned through seven seasons of *The Walking Dead* in one week. *I may not have risen from the dead, son, but I made it to Ohio.*

What Anne failed to mention until they'd passed Toledo was the fact that she'd invited other people for the weekend. They were all fellow therapists, she said. The focus of the weekend was a technique therapists referred to as Constellation Work or more formally as Systemic Family Therapy that Anne had decided Corinne might benefit from as well.

"It's an alternative therapy," Anne explained. "Somewhat unconventional, but very cathartic as a grief management tool."

"Are you kidding me?" Corinne's rage was so intense she felt like she might eject from the passenger seat and catapult into space.

"I knew you'd say no if I told you up front. You have every right to be angry. I promise you don't have to participate; I just want you to think about it. You can take part in the workshops, or, if you don't feel like it, just hang out on the beach or take some long walks. Scott and I talked, and we decided we needed to do something drastic to get you out of the house. I'm well aware that I am crossing a line here, but we both want you to recover."

Corinne could not even speak. Anne had been talking to her son? *On the phone?* So much for appearing cheerful during his visits. Apparently, he had not been fooled by her fake smiles. He had found his mother *pathetic.*

When they arrived at the cottage, Corinne headed straight out to the deck to smoke a cigarette as a *fuck you* to Anne, who had posted No Smoking signs on every available surface at her house and cabin.

The lake was crystalline. Not a cloud in the sky. A line of shorebirds was stationed on the rusty old boat launch. She and Ethan had signed up for a shorebird identification class last year on Belle Isle in Detroit. Now, she peered down at the shorebirds and realized all she had retained were random names: plover, peep, snipe. She could never parse the identifying characteristics: short bills, short legs, short necks, who knew? If Ethan had been there, he would not have been able to help her either. After the second class, he'd turned to her and whispered, "These birds are as indistinguishable as snowflakes." During the coffee break, they'd snuck out of the class and headed to Rose's Diner for breakfast instead.

Way off on the horizon, a freighter glided by, slight as a fingernail file. Back in Detroit on Lake St. Clair, the freighters passed so closely you could see the people on deck. Corinne took a long drag on her cigarette. Ethan had loved visiting Anne's cottage. Last summer, they'd kayaked all the way to a nature preserve two miles to the east, ignoring Anne's warning about storms blowing up unexpectedly on the shallowest of the Great Lakes. On their return trip, they'd battled fierce waves. As they were struggling through a particularly brutal stretch, a drone had appeared over their heads—someone on shore checking their precarious status. When they realized what it was, Ethan had been so annoyed that he'd swatted at it with his oar. "Is it here to record our impending demise?"

When Corinne returned, Anne was standing in the driveway talking to two women who had just pulled up in a white Ford Explorer. The tall, skinny woman with spiky white hair and black glasses held out her hand and said her name was Bryce. The small, portly woman in the grandma sweater and sturdy shoes introduced herself as Bryce's wife, Gretchen. Anne asked how they had heard about the event, and Bryce said they were "constellation groupies." They had just opened a center for LGBTQ youth in Cleveland, and they believed Constellation Work might help the kids who had trust issues, which was, Bryce added, just about all of them.

"You don't even know these people?" Corinne hissed into Anne's ear as they headed inside.

"They're fellow therapists. Doesn't mean I *know* them."

"You sure made it sound like they were *fellows* you knew," Corinne said.

"It's a workshop," Anne said, as if that explained everything.

"I would never do this to you," Corinne said. "*Never.*"

Anne didn't respond for a second. "I would hope that if I were sitting on my couch for months on end and you had tried everything from yoga to barhopping to antiquing and nothing worked, you would not give up on me. You would come up with a plan to save me, no matter the cost to the friendship. At this point, I am more concerned about your well-being than anything else."

Before Corinne could respond, Anne called out to Bryce and Gretchen to follow her up the back staircase. Corinne sat down at the kitchen table.

"I hope you don't mind twin beds. That's all we have in this house," Anne said to the women as they disappeared up the dark stairwell.

"I wish we minded, but sadly, it's not a problem at all," one of them said.

At that, Corinne was hit with another memory of her last visit to the cottage. She and Ethan had stayed in that very same room at the top of the stairs. It was a small room: a former servant's quarter. In the middle of the night, Ethan had tiptoed over to her bed.

"Just like college," he'd whispered. When the ancient bed creaked and moaned, threatening collapse, they'd burst into a fit of giggles. At one point, Corinne had slipped between the bed and the wall and Ethan had had to hoist her back up.

Corinne stared out the kitchen window. Perhaps there was a hotel nearby. She could take a cab and wait out the weekend there. Or she could rent a car and just drive back home.

While she was considering her options, someone knocked on the kitchen door. She opened it to find a tall, bald man with thick black glasses standing in the vestibule. His cheeks were pink and round. He looked like Silly Putty with glasses. Like the lesbian couple, this man, who said his name was Gerard, appeared to be closing in on seventy. Because Anne was still upstairs with Bryce and Gretchen, Corinne had no choice but to converse with him. As he talked, he stooped with his head cocked to the right, though whether to hear better or look sympathetic, Corinne wasn't sure. He said he spent a majority of his time counseling sex addicts, and he'd signed up for the weekend because he was burned out.

"People get stuck," he said.

Did he mean the therapists or the sex addicts? And what did sex addicts get stuck in? Ethan would have come up with a zinger for that one. She'd been the straight man; he'd been the comedian. And what is a straight man without a comedic sidekick? A blank slate.

"Very true," Corinne said to Gerard.

"You'll be really surprised how moving this is," he said. "Last time I did Constellation Work, I cried nonstop."

Great, Corinne thought. *I haven't done that in a while.*

Two hours later, after the rest of the guests had arrived, Anne announced that it was time to get to work, and one by one they all traipsed up the stairs to the second-floor great room. The far wall comprised floor-to-ceiling windows overlooking the lake. Anne had positioned a dozen dining room and folding chairs in a circle in front of the window.

The therapists fanned out: Bryce and Gretchen sat in the farthest corner, followed by Gerard, Anne, Corinne, a young therapist named Ruby, and an older grandmotherly therapist named Estelle, who worked in a halfway house for opioid addicts in Cleveland. Corinne had followed everyone upstairs because she couldn't think of a way to politely decline, and she was curious to see how this all played out. After a decent interval, she planned to say she had a headache and retreat to her room.

The group leaders, Dan and Oona Marks, introduced themselves. They were young, close to Scott's age. They looked like people who either exercised for a living or lived to exercise. Both wore black yoga pants and matching black tops, stomachs iron flat. Oona's red hair was cinched into a ponytail that threatened to splinter her face. Dan reminded Corinne of the hirsute barista at her local Starbucks, the one who looked like he was trying out for a part on *Little House on the Prairie*. One time, when she and Ethan were in Starbucks and she'd dropped a dollar in the tip jar, Ethan had said, "Soon he'll have enough for the butter churn."

Oona and Dan had moved their chairs directly in front of the picture window as if they were deliberately trying to block the view. Beyond them on the rusty dock, the shorebirds continued their vigil. Out of nowhere, Corinne remembered the only fact she had retained from her shorebirds class. Shorebirds congregate on the shores of Lake Erie before migration because they are working up the nerve to traverse the long stretch of open water. "It's the fact that they can't see across the water that stymies them," the instructor had said. "It literally stops them in their tracks until the weather shifts and they have no choice but to brave it."

Dan said he would like to go around the circle for introductions. "I'll start," he said. "Oona and I have been married for five years, and we just started discussing kids. I expect that discussion will take another five years." He looked at Oona, and she rolled her eyes. Everyone half-laughed.

Dan explained that Constellation Work is a tool for uncovering unhealthy family dynamics, which sometimes span generations. It was created by a German man named Bert Hellinger, who had modeled the technique after a tribal ritual he'd witnessed in Africa.

"Essentially," Dan said, "it's role-play. Just think of it as a way to work through your relationship problems via us." He got up from his chair and began walking slowly around the circle with his hands clasped behind his back. "Now, I can't promise everyone will get a turn, but I will try to be fair. Why don't you all tell me a little bit about your issues."

Estelle said she was working with opioid addicts and she was weary of "the endless loop." Gerard admitted that he was tired of his sex-addicted patients, who made him feel profoundly lonely. "I'm old enough that sex has lost its appeal, which doesn't help," he added. "I keep thinking, *just get over it already.*"

Gretchen and Bryce said they thought witnessing each other's constellations would help with some of their long-term relationship issues and more directly connect them to the LGBTQ kids at the center.

Anne said she needed to know how to cope with her workaholic husband.

Ruby said she wanted to cast off the shadow of alcoholism in her family. "I may be the only one who doesn't have it," she said, and then, in an ominous tone, added, "*Yet.*"

When they turned their attention to Corinne, she said she was Anne's guest, and she was just there to observe. Everyone nodded. Corinne couldn't tell if they were nodding to say this was fine and they would let her be, or it was fine for now, but they would make it their mission to draw her out.

After the introductions, Dan patted the rectangular box in his lap, then opened it and produced a small crystal, which he placed on the floor in the middle of the room.

"To ground us," he said.

Corinne fought a smile. She looked over at Anne, but thankfully, Anne was turned the other way.

After he had circled the room a couple times, he stopped in front of Ruby. "I think I'm picking up something right here," he said, using his pointer finger to draw a circle in the air in front of Ruby.

Fearing she might laugh, Corinne fixed her concentration on the window. Another freighter had appeared along the horizon, everyone onboard oblivious to this absurdity.

Ruby said on top of the legacy of alcoholism, she couldn't muster any enthusiasm for her patients, some of whom were suicidal. She was afraid her ennui might prove fatal if she didn't get it under control.

Dan bobbed his head as Ruby explained that her mother had often cut her down when she was drunk, and when she wasn't doing that, she ignored her.

Bobbing is a feature of the solitary sandpiper, Corinne suddenly remembered, surprising herself with a second shore-bird factoid. "Score!" she wanted to yell. If only Ethan were there to give her a high five.

"Can you pick someone to play her?" Dan said when Ruby was finished dismantling her mother.

Ruby pointed to Anne. Dan asked Anne to join them in the center of the room.

"Just place your hands on Anne's shoulders and lead her to the place in the room that you want your mother to occupy," Dan said.

Ruby steered Anne to the far right corner of the room, as far as Anne could go without toppling down the staircase. Then she turned Anne around so that she was facing the window, her back toward the room.

Holy cow, Corinne thought. Ruby must really hate her mother to corner her like that. Scott had gone through a similar phase in tenth grade. Every time she opened her mouth, he'd yell, "Don't talk to me!" Now, Corinne realized that the same dynamic might play out ad infinitum, decades after high school. Great news.

"Now, pick someone to play your maternal grandmother," Dan said.

Corinne tried to avoid catching her eye, but Ruby homed in on her anyway.

When Corinne didn't move, Dan said, "I should have mentioned at the beginning, people who are chosen to be in the constellation can always say no."

Corinne looked at all the therapists staring at her. How could she say no? She was stuck with these nincompoops for the entire weekend. Reluctantly, she got up from her chair.

Ruby placed Corinne at the opposite end of the room, as far as she could possibly be from Anne/mom. And unlike Anne/mom, Corinne/grandma was allowed to face the group instead of the window. She would have preferred to scan for shorebirds than stare out at the circle of therapists who stared back at her beady-eyed, a little like the wake of vultures that lined Anne's deck railing some mornings scouting for carcasses.

Bryce was picked to play Ruby's father, and Ruby positioned her in the middle of the room like the Washington Monument. Gretchen was given the role of Ruby's maternal grandfather, and she was stationed to the left of Bryce.

Typical, Corinne thought, putting the men in the middle.

"Now choose someone to play you, Ruby," Dan said.

There was no one left except the old woman, Estelle. When Ruby motioned to her, Estelle stood up and shuffled onto what Corinne had started to think of as the stage. Ruby placed Estelle directly in front of Bryce.

Dan directed the real Ruby to sit back down on the couch, then he made his way from actor to actor, peering into each face before moving on to the next person.

"The first thing I notice is that Dad here," he pointed to Bryce, "is in the middle of the room. He's taller than everyone else, and he's the only one looking out over the whole gathering. He's the epicenter. Granddad is here to his left, almost as powerful."

"Pop," Ruby said from her chair. "We called him Pop."

"OK. Remember, no interruptions," Dan said to her.

He turned back to the actors. "We have Mom over in the corner just looking out the window, kind of disengaged. She can't even see what's going on. Grandma is way over on the other side of the room, and here's Ruby. Ruby is here with the men. She's put herself in a powerful position."

Dan went over to Anne and said, "How are you feeling, Mom?"

Corinne heard Anne's voice falter. "I'm just so sad over here staring out the window. I can't see my mother. I can't see my daughter. I can't see anyone. And for some reason, knowing that my husband is in the middle of the room is making me absolutely furious."

"Interesting," Dan said.

Corinne glanced over at the real Ruby. She was sitting on the couch cross-legged with her mouth open.

Dan walked over to Bryce. "How are you feeling, Dad?" Dan asked.

"Well, I'm in charge. I'm feeling pretty powerful here in the center of the room, but I can't help feeling sad, too. Everyone is so far away except for Pop here." Bryce pointed her thumb at Gretchen.

"How about you, Pop?" Dan said. "What's going on with you?"

"I feel like my wife doesn't love me. She's standing behind me, way over there in the corner of the room, and she's just staring out the window." Gretchen's voice wavered as if she were about to cry.

"That's not your wife," Dan said. "That's your daughter. Your wife is pretty far away, but she is looking at you."

"Right," Gretchen said. "Well, I'm still pretty ticked off. My daughter won't even look at me. My wife is looking at me, but I can't reach her." At that, she burst into tears.

Corinne looked over at Ruby. Her mouth was still open, tears running down her cheeks.

Gretchen stood in the center of the room, swaying back and forth, crying silently.

This has got to be a joke, Corinne thought.

Even though she tried to will him away, Dan approached her next. "How are you, Grandma?" he asked.

"I keep thinking, what in the world am I doing here?" Corinne said.

Dan nodded his head. "At some point in life, that's a question we all ask ourselves, don't we?"

Next up on the constellation rotation was Gretchen, who had to deal with her religious mother played by Anne. Then Estelle, whose daughter wouldn't speak to her. Estelle positioned her daughter, played by Corinne, in front of her mother, played by Anne, and her grandma/Ruby, like a long line of dominoes.

Corinne's mother had not wanted her to marry Ethan. When Corinne told her that she was getting married, her mother had refused to acknowledge the announcement. Ethan lived in Detroit, and Corinne's mother couldn't imagine Corinne leaving New York City. Why would anyone in their right mind leave New York? And leaving New York had been hard, her mother was right about that. But Corinne had been happy in Detroit, mostly because of Ethan. Now that she could move anywhere she wanted, she didn't think location would make a bit of difference. All the greeting cards were right: home is where the heart is. How sappy and sad was that?

When Dan finally made his way over to Corinne, she said, "Thank you, no. I don't have anything to work on today."

"But I have the feeling you are in pain," Dan said. "Perhaps we can try a different technique?"

He turned to Oona. "Would you be willing?" he asked, tilting his head.

Oona sighed and made a face that suggested she would if forced.

"I think you lost someone recently," Dan said to Corinne.

Corinne looked over at Anne. Anne shrugged and shook her head.

"Yes," Corinne said.

"Oona is a shaman," Dan said. "She may be able to reach . . ." He paused and raised his eyebrows.

"Ethan," Corinne said. "But no, thank you. I don't need to reach him."

Oona stood up and walked over to them. "It might help to be able to speak to him."

"What do you mean speak to him?"

Oona tucked her tiny black T-shirt back into her black leggings. Her legs were as spindly as a sandpiper's. "Sometimes they come through. Sometimes they don't. But we can try."

Everyone stared at Corinne.

"Fine," Corinne said. If worse came to worst, she'd have a good excuse for belting this woman, and, at the very least, she'd have a funny story to tell Scott.

Oona motioned her over to the middle of the room. She sat down on one side of the crystal and told Corinne to sit on the other side.

"Please don't disturb us," Oona said to the group. "I need to remain completely focused."

Oona took Corinne's hands and closed her eyes. Corinne stared at her. It would be awful if she started to laugh. Luckily, she didn't feel like laughing. She didn't know what she felt. A bit of anger, perhaps, that she'd even entertained the thought:

what if this works? Anger that this woman was offering her such false promise. Anger that all the needy people in this room were being duped.

Suddenly Oona wobbled; her eyebrows fluttered, and her entire body shuddered. Her head lowered and her mouth fell open. After a few seconds, she opened her eyes. It looked like she was stoned.

"What's going on?" she asked, blinking slowly. "Where am I?"

If nothing else, Corinne was impressed by Oona's acting job. She had managed to misplace some inner light; she looked as vacant as Corinne's grandmother when the dementia had set in.

Corinne glanced around the room. Anne was perched on the end of her seat as if watching a tennis match. She nodded encouragingly to Corinne.

What was Corinne supposed to say?

"Ethan?" she asked.

"Yes," Oona said in a breathy whisper.

The fact that Oona had answered yes to Ethan's name knocked Corinne flat. The nerve of it. This charade was such an awful thing to do to a grieving person, but when Corinne glanced around the room, everyone appeared enthralled. It was truly unbelievable! How gullible would you have to be to buy this crap? If she got up and walked out, would she crush these people? What did she owe them anyway? How long did she have to play along? Out of frustration or anger—she wasn't sure which—tears started seeping from Corinne's eyes. She swiped at them with her thumb.

"Ethan?" she asked again.

"Where am I?" Oona asked, continuing with her heavy-lidded gaze.

"You're dead," Corinne said. It took everything out of her not to add, *faker*.

"No, I'm not," Oona said, shaking her head slowly. "I'm having trouble waking up this morning. It's too early."

"You're not asleep," Corinne said. As she said it, a hiccup came out. She put a hand up to her mouth. "Excuse me," she said.

"Excuse you," Oona said with a spaced-out smile. "Why didn't you set the alarm?"

"You always set the alarm," Corinne said. *It's a big deal. It involves a lot of discussion.*

"So, why can't I get up today?" Oona said.

"Because you're dead! You're dead! You're dead," Corinne hissed. "You died in your sleep. You never woke up!"

From one of the chairs, Corinne heard a gasp.

"I died?" Oona said.

"Yes. You finally got to sleep in! Isn't that great news? No more yoga!" Corinne laughed, and even to her the laugh sounded hysterical.

Oona shook her head slowly, as if she couldn't quite accept it or wasn't hearing correctly or didn't know what to say next. *Of course she doesn't know what to say next; she's a fraud.*

"At least you don't have to get up to exercise anymore, Iron Man," Corinne continued. "At least you're done answering to the Axman. At least you don't have to squeegee the second-floor windows this spring. At least you don't have to pay for that roof renovation. And just think—no more kale."

Oona nodded slowly. "True," she smiled. "That was gross."

How long could Oona remain unflappable? Corinne decided to kick it up a notch.

"You can eat whatever you want. You can wear your poodle pants all day long. I won't force you to learn the rumba. M&M heaven, am I right?"

"My poodle pants." Oona nodded and smiled.

Corinne glanced over at Anne. Anne was frowning. What in the world were poodle pants? And Ethan despised M&M's. His little sister had choked once on a peanut M&M. He was the one who'd signed up for the rumba class. He loved dancing. If he'd been in the room, he would have been howling, but Corinne did not think any of this was funny.

"At least you won't get caught again," Corinne continued.

"Say what?" Oona said.

"You remember—when the maid caught you in the bathroom with those girlie magazines?"

Oona's mouth opened and closed a couple of times like one of Ethan's giant goldfish, the ones who persevered despite abject neglect.

"I think I see something," Oona said, finally. "It's a light coming at me."

"That might be the light from the maid opening the door. Remember when she walked in? You were so embarrassed, but you shouldn't have been. It's natural. Well . . . maybe not the scissors. Maybe not the Cheerios and the toothpaste."

Oona nodded. "But I think I have to go now . . . I think I should go into that light."

"Lots of people have outlandish proclivities. There was the man who taped himself to a light pole and the one who liked to hang upside down from the rafters like a bat. The old notions of sin are a thing of the past. I don't think St. Peter's going to block your way. I don't think you should be frightened."

"I *was* a little frightened," Oona said.

Oona said this with such intensity that Corinne was jolted briefly out of her game.

"When?" she asked.

"When I died."

"I thought you said you were asleep."

"I was afraid when I couldn't wake up. It felt like the really bad kind of morning when you just can't drag yourself out of bed. And then I realized I couldn't move."

"Huh." Corinne didn't know when she had ever been more furious. "You'd think after all those downward dogs . . . Hell, I'm the smoker. I'm the one who can't hold a plank for five seconds. I'm the one who should have dropped dead. Not you, Iron Man."

Oona nodded again. "You're joking," she said, gravely. "You do that."

"We do that," Corinne said, jabbing her finger at Oona and then at herself. "We do that! Or we did, anyway."

Oona nodded again. "I think I should go now," she said.

"Bye-bye." Corinne waggled her fingers. "See you on the flip side."

When Corinne returned to her chair, Dan suggested they all take a couple of minutes to meditate. The other participants closed their eyes, possibly trying to block out the light.

"Let's hold hands," Dan said.

"You know what?" Corinne said. "I need some air."

When Corinne reached the dock, she lit a cigarette and stared out at the water. The shorebirds hadn't budged.

"You're going to have to move on at some point!" she yelled. A couple of the smaller birds flapped their wings at the noise, but in the end, they remained nonplussed.

It had all been so ludicrous, but strangely, she did feel a bit better. Sitting across from Oona, the shaman, with that crazy, empty look on her face, it had occurred to Corinne that she and Ethan had been like two shorebirds in a long line of shorebirds—on the surface it would have been impossible for Oona or anyone else to pick out a characteristic that set them apart. But Corinne knew all the identifying features, behaviors, sounds. Their thing—whatever they'd had—was worth a whole class. It was worth a *study*. She took a few more drags and then crushed out her cigarette.

She felt energized. She would go back inside and ask for her turn doing the Constellation Work. She would place every single one of the therapists on the stage. One would be Ethan peering out the window, and one would be Ethan standing like a monument in the middle of the room, and one would be Ethan toppling the other dominoes, and one would be the Ethan who was just sitting on the couch laughing along with her.

She imagined circling the room pointing to Bryce and Gretchen and Estelle and Ruby:

You be Ethan and you be Ethan and you be Ethan.

JUNGLE LIFE

When my father started forgetting things—the name of his favorite restaurant, whether he'd paid the gas bill, how he'd ended up in Victoria's Secret way out at the Oakland Park Mall—we took him to Dr. Gray, who gave us that familiar devastating diagnosis. Before we left his office, he caught hold of my arm. "I always tell the kids this: Think of his mind as a library on fire. Take advantage of the time you have left."

He suggested I interview my father and record it.

I was twenty-one, my father sixty-six. He hadn't married until he was forty-three, long after his brother and most of his friends. Given my age and the plight of the world at the time—it was the height of the Gulf War, and my friends and I spent every night huddled around the TV—I latched on to his World War II stories from the Pacific. I'm ashamed to say, I didn't pay much attention to the rest. Years later, I did go back and review the tapes for subjects that were becoming pertinent to my own life: marriage, kids, business concerns. But at the time, like most guys my age, the battle tales fascinated me.

We always took a back booth at the Cozy Diner during

our recording sessions, and now I'm sorry. The background noise—music, clattering plates, Maureen the waitress's raucous laughter—made some parts of the recording unintelligible. My other regret is that I didn't use video.

Looking at my white-haired father hunkered over the table in his Cleveland Indians baseball cap and windbreaker, it was hard to fathom that he had been in New Guinea when he was my age, living in the jungle, picking off body lice, and trying to keep his feet from molding.

For our first four recording sessions that was all I got out of him: jungle life sucked.

"We all had this foot fungus, gosh did it ever itch. If you left your shoes on the floor of your tent, by morning they were covered in mold. And then there were leeches. You'd come back to camp and they'd just be stuck to you like huge jelly pods. We didn't have toothpaste; my gums were so sore that drinking water was painful. One time I used this leaf for toilet paper and my rear end oozed for weeks."

The fifth time, when he started up on bugs and culinary anomalies, I stopped him.

"But did you ever actually do anything?" I said. "Were you ever in combat?"

"Sure, sure," he said and took a sip of his coffee.

Just then, Maureen appeared with the #1: two scrambled eggs, rye toast, and hash browns for one dollar and ninety-nine cents.

"Who ordered this?" he said.

Maureen glanced at me, her penciled brows arched. We'd been ordering the exact same thing every Saturday for as long as I could remember.

"You did," I said.

"Oh."

He took his fork and poked at the eggs. Then he picked up the toast and turned it over, examining both sides. He never told me that the meal was as new to him as the stories in that morning's edition of the *Saline Gazette*, but it was clear from the look on his face. Now, I realize how terrifying that must have been for him.

"So, the combat?" I asked.

"Sure."

"You know, Dad, I'd like to hear about that. I'd be interested in that."

"Well," he said, "I spent the fall of 1944 in the jungles of New Guinea."

"We got that far."

"We were fighting the Japanese, and when I landed in New Guinea, the fighting had been going on for quite a while. In fact, my understanding was that for all intents and purposes we had already won. Nevertheless, every so often, they'd send two or three of us out into the jungle on scouting missions.

"So, one day, I was sent in with a guy named Stanton. I hardly knew him. All I remember is he used to crack us all up lighting his farts on fire. Anyway, we were headed up the Kokoda Trail. We walked for about an hour slashing our way through this thick, coarse undergrowth with our machetes. The grass was seven feet high in places, and that boggy ground just sucked you down. It smelled horrible. There were times the climb was so steep I had to hold onto roots and pull myself up the path. When we finally broke through to a clearing, we were covered in leeches."

"You've told me about the leeches," I interrupted. I didn't want him sidetracked again.

"I still remember how beautiful it was there," my dad continued, "just a wide-open field of ferns. Electric green. And the butterflies! Every color under the sun. It was so peaceful. I remember thinking, 'I could stay here forever.' The sunlight was pushing through the canopy like fingers.

"Anyway, we picked off the leeches. Then we sat down to rest against two trees. Stanton was sitting across from me. We were both dozing, and the next thing I knew there was this strange noise. A high-pitched squeal like a cat held upside down by its tail. I looked over at Stanton. Turned out he was making the noise. He was staring straight ahead. Frozen. A large knife protruding from the trunk about an inch above his head. Looking across the clearing, I saw nine or ten tribesmen staring at him. Spears and knives pointed right at him. I didn't think. I just reacted. I got up, grabbed my machete and ran. Didn't have a clue what he was doing, just kept running, couldn't stop. They didn't come after us. There was no noise behind me, and before I knew it, I had reached camp. After I finished telling the guys what had happened, there was this thrashing from the bush and out comes Stanton, terrified. He didn't say a word when he saw everyone, just leaned over and vomited right there on the spot. Afterward, he refused to speak. He just walked past everyone, went into his tent, and never came out again. I never saw him again. I suppose they shipped him home at some point.

"But," he added, "the thing that stuck with people—the thing that still sends a chill up my own spine—is that when

Stanton emerged from the jungle, his hair had turned completely white."

"That isn't possible," I said.

"I know it, but it's true."

He said he wouldn't have believed it either if he hadn't seen it with his own eyes.

My recorder suddenly turned off. I asked him to wait a minute.

While I was fiddling with the tape, he coughed and said he was sorry I had to witness his "descent into dementia." I mumbled something about being sorry he had to go through it. I felt horribly panicky and had trouble meeting his eye. Maureen was pouring Father Andrew's coffee. A couple of my buddies were devouring pancakes over in the corner. When they saw me looking over at them, they waved. My calf muscles started twitching. I had to hold onto the table to keep from popping up out of my seat.

"You know," he said, pushing away his uneaten breakfast. "They say that which doesn't kill you makes you stronger, but I haven't always found that to be the case. I suppose you're better off holding on to the way we used to be. When I get really bad, pretend like I'm already gone."

"Dad!"

"I'm serious. Remember the good times," he said. "Forget the rest."

"OK. OK," I said. "Tell me about the car dealership."

When he got back from the war, he worked for a Ford dealership, and just before I was born, he bought the owner out. While he talked, I thought up a long string of questions:

his years as county commissioner, how he met my mother, winning Saline Man of the Year. Anything to keep him from going morbid on me. Now that I'm older, I'd give anything to do that whole conversation over again.

The next time we sat down, a week later, I said, "OK. Let's get back to the war. You were telling me about the jungle. Remember? About the time you and Stanton were doing recon."

"Right," he said, leaning toward the tape recorder. "He was a great guy. Probably my best buddy. We'd been together since Hawaii. In fact, we'd been together so long we even had this dog back on Maui—a German Shepherd named Scout. We were always going to go back and get him."

He stopped and gazed out the window. Maureen brought over our plates. This time he didn't seem confused by the transaction. He talked while he ate, which is why this section of the recording sounds garbled. I transcribed it that night so I wouldn't forget what he said. How he ate while he was telling this story, I'll never know.

"We had just crossed this enormous mountain range. We were covered with leeches, and we were starving, and we'd gone from freezing to death at the top to neck deep in swamp on the way back down. We had to follow these steep ridges all the way up, and I remember one time this guy named Ralph Donaldson slipped and then we all slid down, must have been one thousand feet. It took us about eight hours to climb back up. All the while, people are sick and dying of malaria and dysentery. We were the walking dead. The food! They gave us these tins of Australian bully beef that nearly killed us all. By the time we reached the other side, we had lost a lot of steam and a lot of equipment. When we got there, we thought there were maybe fifteen hundred of them, but we found out later there were more than six thousand. And they handled the terrain better. They built these bunkers that we could never see until we were right on top of them. We used to have to crawl around, and when we found one, we'd jam a hand grenade into one of the firing slits.

"One time I went in with Stanton. At that point we thought we were seven or eight miles from the Japs. It turned out we were wrong. Anyway, we were cutting our way through the jungle, and we came to a clearing. Out of nowhere, a shot rings out and catches Stanton in the chest. I looked around, but I couldn't see anything. Next thing I know, bullets are raining down on me, so I turn and hightail it back to camp. Later that day, I led everyone back in. When we got to the clearing, we simply circumvented it, and that way we were able to ambush them."

"What about Stanton?"

"Well, we found him in the bunker."

"He was dead?"

"Oh, yes. I knew he was dead. They hit him square in the chest. That wasn't the worst part."

"What could be worse?"

"It's hard to even say it . . ."

He pushed his scrambled eggs around on his plate.

"They'd eaten him," he said.

"What?"

"I remember vomiting right there on the spot. I wasn't the only one either."

"That's unbelievable. What did you all do . . . after that?"

"I looked for a letter for his wife, any personal stuff, but there was nothing. They probably burned it all. Then we had to figure out what to do with him, and for a lot of reasons, we couldn't move him. We were weak from sickness and hunger ourselves, and well, we didn't want to attract more of them. I said some prayers over him, and when we got back to camp, I wrote to his wife and his parents."

"That's a far cry from the story you told me before," I said.

"I told you this story before?" he said.

Later that spring, my father became incontinent and took to wandering the neighborhood at night searching in the shrubs for some "thing" he could never remember when we found him. My mother and I took him to the Mt. Carmel Nursing Home one hot day in late May. That summer, I helped her clean out the house—not just his bedroom—the whole house. Visiting my father, my mother was candy cane sweet, but at night she tore through the bureaus and closets upending drawers and emptying cupboards, raving about everything from the Channel Four weatherman's earring to the high price of coffee to the scratchy sheets my father complained about at the Home. Her rage had no parameters.

One night she even called Carnival Cruise Line and lit into them because they sent several pamphlets advertising the cruise my parents had planned on taking when she retired.

By mid-August, we could have been living at the Holiday Inn. There was no sign that we had ever inhabited the house. I joked about putting a packet of soap in the bathroom and sticking a vacancy sign in the window. I couldn't tease so much as a smile out of her.

All that last summer of my father's life, I thought about Stanton. Which story was true? Every time I visited him at the Home, I tried to find the right moment to bring it up. Often, I came in to find him sitting in his pea-green armchair, staring out the window. When I sat down opposite him, he'd say, "Hi, how are you?" with a big inflection on "you."

It reminded me of the greeting you might get from a celebrity or a politician who knows he's met you before but can't quite place you. Even after the generic welcome, I sat there hoping he would reemerge. Usually if the day started out poorly, things only got worse. His favorite exclamation was, "That's baseball!" which he sometimes shouted over and over until a nurse came in and sedated him. A couple of times when I told him to stop, he started yelling even louder just to annoy me, as if he were a six-year-old taunting his older brother. On these occasions, my mother fled to the cafeteria. For my part, I often looked into the mirror over his bureau half expecting my own hair to have lost all its pigment.

He had been in the Home for two months when I finally intercepted a cogent moment. He was sitting in his chair talking to a big, tattooed Hells Angels–type janitor about the Cleveland Indians. He seemed to be following the conversation.

After he left and my father had asked about my mother's cat, Reggie, I figured it was now or never.

"Dad," I said, "do you remember Stanton?"

"Stanton?"

"Your friend . . . from the war?"

"Why would you bring him up?"

"You told me about him, remember?"

"Me? I didn't . . ." He leaned forward in his chair. "She sent you, didn't she?"

"Who?"

"There was no letter! Tell her to leave me alone."

"Who?"

He covered his face with his gnarled hands. His shoulders began to shake. Not even a minute had passed since I'd brought up Stanton, and my father was distraught.

"Dad, forget it. I'm sorry I said anything about it."

He rocked back and forth. Small noises rose from the back of his throat. I was sure a nurse would come in and yell at me. I got up from my chair and went over to him, laying a hand on his shoulder. I wasn't sure what to say.

"Dad, forget it. It happened so long ago."

"Why do you keep saying that?" He wiped his right eye with his index finger. "He was my best friend. I should have gone back."

THE DEVIL'S PROOF

In the mid-eighties, I attended an all-girls Catholic preparatory school in Washington, D.C. Safety, both corporeal and spiritual, was the nuns' number one priority. Nothing was going to happen to any of the girls on their watch. Every morning after we arrived, the security guard we had nicknamed Gollum locked the wrought-iron gate with an enormous key that hung from a thick rope around his neck. Then he hobbled with his skeleton head cane back to his security post, a small brick building in the middle of the parking lot, where he watched various sporting events until the end of the day when it was time to set us free. If it had not been for his German Shepherd, Rolf, he would never have noticed when we made a break for it.

Despite the nuns' vigilance, by sophomore year most of the girls in my class were schooled in the romantic arts. The ones who said they had "gone all the way" were the same girls who knew how to apply makeup and arrived at school Madonna-chic, striding down the corridors in alluring, scornful packs. During study hall, they offered tutorials, and the rest of us—naïve and mortified by it—listened with rapt attention. Decades passed before I realized the fact that they omitted the more diabolical encounters probably meant that despite their sophisticated veneers, they were every bit as unschooled as me.

I was young for my grade. The fall of my junior year, I was still fifteen. My parents were battling at that point, effectively separated. They refused to get divorced for religious reasons, but my mother had opened a travel agency, and she told everyone that "field work" set her apart from the competition. Her numerous trips meant that she was gone about twenty weeks out of every year. My father spent the nights when she was in town living in a guest room at Congressional Country Club way out in Maryland. When she was out in the field, he moved back home to take care of me.

The Exorcist was shown on television the first year of my parents' new living arrangement. My father was home that evening, and we watched it together in our small wood-paneled study with my father's solitary Duraflame log blazing in the fireplace.

I'd grown up with a Catholic fear of the Devil, but I had no idea that he could just decide to lodge inside a person against her will. It sounds melodramatic to say it, but nevertheless it's true: that movie changed the trajectory of my life. Midway through, as Regan projectile vomited, I attempted a joke to relieve my escalating anxiety.

"I'm so glad the Devil hasn't gotten to any of my friends yet," I said.

"Me too," my father said. "But it does happen. This is based on a true story. I went to Georgetown University with the guy who wrote the book."

According to my father, Bill Blatty had learned about the exorcism in a religion class at Georgetown. In the movie, the possessed girl was just a sweet, happy-go-lucky kid, but in real life, my father said that the demon had taken hold of a troubled boy. The priest who performed the real exorcism had lived through the experience. He had not ended up at the bottom of a steep staircase like the one who performed the exorcism in the movie.

"Still, how do you know it's really true?" I asked.

"The guy who performed the exorcism was the same one teaching our class," he said without looking away from the TV.

"No way!" I said, then sat silently staring at the fire. The Duraflame glowed red and yellow and I imagined seeing the Devil pop out from behind it without warning.

He glanced at me, possibly alarmed by my silence. "It happened, but no need to worry," he said. "I believe it's very rare."

He said this with a small smile that to me looked like sadness more than anything. It was the *we will survive* smile, and I had seen it many times since the separation was announced.

"Thanks a lot, Dad. I will never get over this."

"No need to worry," he said, as he harrumphed his way up out of his chair. "Just don't give the Devil an opening. Stay away from Ouija Boards."

The Exorcist had been filmed in Georgetown, where I lived. I had been jogging up the infamous steps numerous times during tennis practice. One reviewer dubbed it "the scariest movie ever made," and that person couldn't see the Gothic spires of Healy Hall from their bedroom window. It was like learning Freddy Krueger was based on the serial killer who grew up two doors down and had never been caught.

I couldn't stop thinking about it. I couldn't sleep.

Like my father, my mother told me not to worry. "If you go to confession every week, the Devil will never gain purchase, Marie," she said. The following Saturday, she took me to confession at Holy Trinity Church. I went on my own for several Saturdays after that.

In the mornings on the way to school, I stopped strolling leisurely down P Street, past Neam's Market and Thomas Sweet Ice Cream Parlor. Instead, I ran at top speed, tripping repeatedly over the bulging, uneven cobblestones. I regularly fell asleep in class because I'd taken up all-night surveillance on the floor in front of my bedroom door beside my Jack Russell Terrier, Mavis.

I remained in this state for several weeks until one day, when we were walking into English class, my friend Sue said, "I'm sick of you moping around with those dark circles under your eyes. Have you seen your hair? You look like a total basket case."

I sat down in my seat and turned toward the front of the room. Sister Veronica started running on about Chaucer. I was annoyed. Didn't Sue realize that I would have given anything to toss my fear in the trash like used Kleenex? It was not that simple.

Several minutes later, Sue passed me a note. It said she was bored and we should skip out after math, head down to Healy Pub. In those days, the drinking age was eighteen. Though we were fifteen, no one ever carded us. Healy Pub was in the basement of Georgetown University, and we were frequent visitors.

Sue's life revolved around locating the next party. Her parents didn't figure into the equation. She might have occupied the same house as her timid mother, but it was like sharing space with a mouse. As for her father—he had once put Sue's head through a wall. There was still a big hole above the couch in the living room to prove it. She had absorbed his rage and seemed lit from within with animosity. She was tall and thin. She wore her long blonde hair in a tight ponytail. Her light blue eyes were piercing, and though I don't think she realized she was doing it, people sometimes asked her why she was glaring at them.

As Sister Veronica droned on, Sue passed me another note: *Before we head to the Pub, we're going to the steps, and we're going to Linda Blair's house. You're going to look your demons in the eye.*

The best way to ditch school was to leave the academic building by the back door and slip into the Senior Lodge. The Lodge was a redbrick cabin located behind the cloisters next to the area where the contemplative nuns resided. It was rumored to have sheltered runaway slaves during the Civil War. The leaded glass windows still sported names and dates (the earliest: 1802) etched into the panes with former students' diamond engagement rings.

Once we were in the Lodge, we checked to make sure that no nuns were strolling through the courtyard or sitting on the garden benches fumbling with their beads. When the coast was clear, we crossed to the back door, ran alongside the high stone cloister wall, and then leapt over the chain-link fence that separated our campus from Georgetown University. As we ran, we listened for the sound of the high-pitched yaps that would mean Rolf had sensed a breach and alerted Gollum. Whenever an escapee was apprehended by Gollum and Rolf, she had to spend several weekends scrubbing the wood floors with a toothbrush or washing dishes for the nuns in the refectory.

Sue had enlisted another friend, Connie, to come with us. Connie's mother was suffering from breast cancer and would die of it later that year, but Connie never brought it up. If someone asked her, she always said that her mother was doing really well. But inevitably, at some point during any given night she would weep. Connie wore thick Coke-bottle glasses at school but never when she might encounter a boy. At parties she could never tell who was approaching until the person was right in her face.

That day, Sue, Connie, and I made it to the fence without incident. We shed our uniforms and donned our microminis behind the magnolia tree at the far end of the Georgetown University campus. Connie took off her glasses and put them in her backpack. Then—instead of hightailing it down to Healy Pub like we usually did—we sauntered across the main quad simulating what we imagined to be the coed strut. By the time we reached Prospect Street, it had started to sleet. The sky had been gray all day, but now the clouds were racing like cyclists across the sky. The wind's icy fingers reached up our miniskirts. I followed Sue to the top of the steps. She and Connie were standing in the spot where the police examiners had looked down on Burke's twisted head. In the movie, when Regan flings her babysitter Burke Dennings out of the window and down the steps, it had scared me more than the final fall of Father Karras. Father Karras was strong; he had conquered the Devil. But poor Burke was drunk. He was an innocent victim who everyone immediately assumed was careless and responsible for his own death.

Peering down the steps, I felt like I couldn't breathe.

Suddenly there was a loud noise behind us. Feet. Running.

"AAAhhh!" someone yelled.

I crouched into a ball, my hands over my head.

When I peeked out, I saw that three boys were running at us across Prospect Street with their arms stretched out, monster-like, over their heads.

"Vat are you doing at ze steps?" one of them yelled.

"You want I should push you?" another shouted.

"Stop it!" Sue yelled.

I poked my head out. She was pointing frantically at me.

The boys came over and formed a semicircle around me.

One of them looked like Peter Brady, the cute middle brother in *The Brady Bunch*. He held out a hand, and I took hold of it to steady myself as I stood up.

"Her father went to school with Bill Blatty," Connie said.

"No shit!" Peter Brady said. "He lived in my dorm."

"She saw *The Exorcist*, and now she's obsessed with the Devil."

"The Devil doesn't exist," the blond boy said.

"Untrue!" Peter Brady said. "Remember the Devil's proof."

"What's that?" the redhead asked.

"Well, we have some evidence that he exists—like demons and exorcisms and whatnot—but we have no evidence that proves he doesn't exist. It would be impossible to prove that.

People call something that's impossible to prove the Devil's proof."

"Huh," the redhead said.

"Don't hurt your brain, lug head." Peter Brady smacked the redhead on the arm and then turned to me. "So, do you want to see Bill Blatty's room?"

Before I could answer, Sue said, "Yes, she does! This girl has got to face her demons!"

Peter Brady lived in Copen Hall. I don't remember his real name, if I ever knew it. The other two boys lived in the same dorm. The redhead was a basketball player and knew Patrick Ewing, which impressed us.

The dormitory was located on the east end of campus overlooking the Potomac River.

Sue, Connie, and I followed the guys up the stairs. Peter led us up to room number sixty-six.

"No fucking way," Sue said. "You are totally shitting us. He lived in room sixty-six?"

The blond laughed. "You guys look like babies. How old are you?"

"We're freshmen at Mount Vernon," Connie said, winking at me. Mount Vernon, a women's college off Foxhall Road, was right across the street from Connie's house.

We continued down the hall to the common room, where six or seven kids were sitting around a television watching *Guiding Light*. All the furnishings were brown. The room smelled like alcohol and dirty socks. Half-eaten pizza, crumpled paper napkins, and beer cans littered every surface.

Before the separation, my mother never let me watch any television. She used to make me read for an hour every day after school. Now that she was traveling, all her cautious parenting had come to a full stop. I knew exactly what was going on in *Guiding Light* because I taped every episode on our VCR. At that moment, I longed to be home watching it on my basement couch rather than standing in a damp room with a bunch of drunk older boys. Though they were only freshmen, they seemed far more grown-up and intimidating than the high school boys we usually hung out with.

"Is this thing still tapped?" Peter walked over to the keg next to the pool table.

Sue and I sat down at a card table. Peter brought us beer, and we started playing quarters.

"We can't stay long," Connie said to Sue. "I have field hockey."

Sue glanced down at her watch. "We'll stay until three."

I looked down at my watch. It was 1:30 p.m.

Connie followed the blond over to the pool table. Peter asked me if I wanted to see his room so that I could get an idea of where Bill Blatty lived.

Sue raised her eyebrows, and when Peter turned away, she gave me the thumbs up.

It was a typical dorm room: two desks, two chairs, a bunk bed, two chests of drawers. From the window I could just see the corner of Key Bridge. The river was starting to ice over, but the current was fighting it.

Peter said his roommate was out studying.

"He's always studying," he added, lighting a cigarette. "Doesn't know how to have fun."

This reminded me of something my father had once said. One night after he'd had a long, drawn-out argument with my mother, he'd come into my room. When he saw me studying, he said I should try to balance all the work with fun, because later on, when I was an adult, things were going to go south.

Peter sat down at one desk, and I sat down at another. We smoked. At one point he went out to get more beer, and I watched ice chunks bobbing down the river.

I was proud of myself for being brave and hanging out with an eighteen-year-old, but instead of growing accustomed to the arrangement, by 2:15 p.m. I was so nervous I'd drained two and a half beers. I started to feel like I was a part of the chair. A nap sounded good, but I couldn't imagine crossing the room to get to the bed. I remember noticing with astonishment that the sun had broken through the clouds. It felt like someone had injected my head with foam.

We talked for a long time, but the only thing I recall about our conversation (probably because I now think this pertinent) was that his mother was an alcoholic. Once he had come home from school to find her passed out naked in the kitchen.

"An avocado in her hand," he said. "Lettuce all over the floor."

"That must have been weird," I said.

"More than weird. I had a couple of guys with me. It was pretty embarrassing."

He came over and pulled me up out of the chair.

"You look like you're about to nod off." He led me over to the bottom bunk and then sat down beside me. He leaned over to kiss me, but every time we shifted, he hit his head on the upper bunk's metal bed frame. After a few minutes, he used that as an excuse to push me down to a horizontal position. I had only kissed one boy up until that point, and that had been just a brief peck outside an ice-skating rink.

As his tongue flicked across my teeth, I had no idea how to respond, so I simply opened my mouth and let my tongue dart in and out. After two or three minutes I sat back up.

"I'm feeling bad about this."

"About what?"

"Lying down on your bed and all . . ."

"What? What do you want to do . . . stand?" He laughed, but I could tell he wasn't happy.

I noticed that he was looking toward me, not at me. His gaze rested on the wall behind my head. I turned and saw the framed eight-by-ten black-and-white picture of Jesus looking sad and pointing to his heart.

I turned back toward him and he pushed me down again. I tried to get up.

"I'll tell you what: I can understand if you don't want to do more. That's fine. Why don't we just pretend?"

He pushed me down and climbed on top of me fully clothed. I could feel the point of his penis as he ground it into me. He started slowly, but soon he was banging away so violently I felt like one of those squishy bathtub whales, all the beer I'd consumed that afternoon threatening to fountain out of my mouth. My mother had told me that boys can't control themselves and that if I got myself into a bad situation, it was my fault. In light of that, I couldn't think of anything to do but wait for it to end. After a little while, he shuddered and stopped. Then he disembarked and left the room. He did not look back. He didn't say goodbye or thank you or I'll see you later. It felt like the bed was still moving, so I got up. I was still fully clothed, but my miniskirt and shirt were askew. I adjusted them before leaving the room.

The hall was clear. I hurried down to the bathroom and made it to the stall just in time. After I was done puking, I washed my face and hands and returned to the common room to look for Sue and Connie.

When I got there, Connie was sitting on the floor by the back wall smoking a cigarette. A tear was running down the right side of her face. I walked past her and took a seat at the card table. Sue was playing pool, but after a few minutes, she came over and sat down next to me.

"How're you holding up?" she asked.

I told her I wanted to go home, but she said she just needed a minute to sober up. I asked her for a smoke. The room was spinning, and I thought it might help. She tossed her pack to me and returned to the pool table.

"Is that you, Marie?" Connie squinted up at me. For fun, Sue sometimes refused to respond to Connie's myopic inquiries. This time I let her off the hook.

"It's me," I said.

There were more kids in the room now—most of them on the couch watching *General Hospital*. Everyone had a beer in hand. One guy was sitting at a lone desk and appeared to be studying. Red wandered over and offered me another beer. Someone brought in a boom box and started playing the Grateful Dead. Someone else yelled that they couldn't hear the TV, and the guy with the boom box told him to fuck off. Connie asked me how it was going with Peter.

I told her I'd gone to his room and we'd made out.

"Score," she said. "High five!"

I high-fived her. The long ash on her cigarette broke off and fell to the ground, but she didn't see it.

Eventually the guy at the desk stood up and announced that he was heading to class. No one reacted, but it created a domino effect. A couple of guys who'd been glued to the couch got up and left the room. Peter came in and started playing pool with the redhead. Connie held her watch up to her nose.

"Shit," she said. "School's out. I'm supposed to be at field hockey."

"Looks like we've got a couple of hours to kill," Sue said. "You can't play hockey in the state you're in."

Sue, of course, had nothing to do and no reason to be anywhere else. I didn't either. Between her crazy parents and mine, if we were pushed down *The Exorcist* stairs, it might take days for anyone to even notice we were missing.

"Field hockey ends at 5:30," Connie said. "We have to be back by then, at least. My mom's picking me up."

Peter walked over and sat down next to Connie. The redhead brought us more drinks. Connie started crying about her mother, and the redhead wiped her tears away. I had fixed my gaze intently on the television, but I could see Peter staring at me out of the corner of my eye.

He got up.

"Join me," he said, holding out his hand.

I couldn't think of anything I'd rather do less.

"I need to talk to my friend first," I said.

I dragged Connie down the hall to the bathroom.

I told her I wanted to go home. She was leaning into the sink studying her own reflection in the mirror. Her eyeliner had dripped down into fang marks. She took a wet towel and attempted to clean herself up. When she turned around to look at me, her eyes were bright red and the liner had formed wings that extended from the corners of her eyes to her hairline.

"Don't be a dumbass." She took a cigarette out of her purse. Her hand trembled so violently that I had to light the cigarette for her.

"This is the moment you've been waiting for," she said, inhaling deeply. "Life is short. I should know."

"He's a weirdo," I said. "It was terrible."

"Well, you never have to see him again. Just have some fun."

"It's not fun. I just told you, it was terrible."

"That's because you don't know what you're doing yet. You have to practice. Work it. Work it. Work it." She attempted a dance move from an Olivia Newton-John video, but she didn't see the trash can and she stumbled into it, banging her head on the towel dispenser.

Peter was waiting for me when we emerged from the bathroom.

"Join me?" he said, holding out his hand.

Just then, Sue appeared, slipping past us to enter the bathroom. I followed her back in and stood outside her stall.

"Help me," I said. "Get me out of here."

"Seal the deal. I don't know why you're being such a prude."

"I'm not."

She emerged from the stall and headed over to the mirror.

"Listen," I said. "He held me down and just ground away on me. It was disgusting."

"He's frustrated." She fluffed her hair and pulled a lipstick out of the pocket of her jeans. "They all get like that. And who could blame him? You led him on."

"It's bullshit. I'm not having fun, and I'm going home."

When I exited the bathroom, he was still standing there. I let out a small shriek.

"I can be a really nice guy," he said. "I don't think I've proven that to you. This time we'll just talk. I promise."

Sue had followed me out and was standing behind me. "Go ahead, you freak!" she said, pushing me gently toward him.

I returned to his room. This is the point in this story where I'd like to offer some excuse. But there is no excuse. I went back.

This time, after a prolonged make out session, he forced my head between his legs. I had attended enough tutorials in the Lodge to know what was expected of me, but no one had mentioned anything about the unpleasant sensation of having one's head forced down between a boy's legs. The cool girls had always maintained that fellatio was the preferred outcome: consummation for the boy; 100 percent effective birth control for the girl. They hadn't mentioned anything about gagging.

While I was wondering how to get out of the situation, someone opened the door.

Peter let go of my head. I pulled back and scooted down to the other end of the bed. A boy stood in the doorway staring down at us.

"Sorry," the boy said. He turned around, shutting the door behind him.

Peter grabbed hold of my shirt and pulled me back toward

him. I said I had to go. He held on to my shirt and reached up under my skirt. I pressed my hands down over his, trying to push them away.

"I don't want that," I said.

"Yes, you do." He grabbed my wrist with one hand and my tights with the other, yanking them down to my ankles. I tried to get up, but he had maneuvered his knee between my legs and was lying on top of me, using his body weight to pin me to the bed.

It all seemed to happen at once. The hands, the penetration, his hot breath. I said stop. Not because I realized he was doing something wrong, but because I could not handle the pain. The bed moved back and forth, up and down. At some point the picture of Jesus crashed to the floor. When I heard the glass shatter, I realized I really had summoned the Devil. He flipped me over onto my stomach and ground my face into the mattress. I stopped struggling because it hurt less when I was still. I don't know how long it continued after that before someone else opened the door.

"What's going on in here?" the person said.

Peter sat up. I was still face down, but I quickly rolled over and reached for the covers, wrapping them around my waist. I stood up, hitting my head on the metal rim of the top bunk, and saw that it was Peter's roommate standing in the doorway. I don't know why he came back. All these years later, I still wonder what he made of the scene.

I ran out of the room, down the hall, down the stairs, out of the building, and across the field with the thin bedcover wrapped around my waist. I don't remember if anyone saw me. It was still light out, so I must have passed other people. I ran to the fence where we'd left our backpacks. I dropped the cover on the ground and adjusted my clothing. Then, I ran the whole ten blocks home, where my mother had just gotten off the phone with Sister Veronica.

I was grounded for three months for skipping my afternoon classes and hopping the fence. Connie was grounded for a while too, but then her mother died. Sue didn't get in any trouble at home. Her mother had missed Sister Veronica's call, and Sue had erased the message. In lieu of suspension, the three of us spent the next three weekends scrubbing the school's wooden porch floors with toothbrushes. Later that year, Sue hopped the fence again and was expelled.

Though I had been going to confession regularly before Peter, I didn't return afterward because I could not imagine telling the priest what I had done. Some weeks later, my class was sent down to the chapel for a special confession. It was unusual to have a priest on campus offering confession. It must have been a Holy Day. When I entered the cubicle, the hot dank air felt like hands all over my body. The priest slid the screen open.

"Forgive me Father, for I have sinned," I said. "It has been two months since my last confession."

"Go ahead," he said.

"I've lied to my mother and I didn't clean up the kitchen when she asked me to. Also, I argued with her. And with my dad a couple of times. I'm sorry."

After, I finished, there was a long pause. I watched the priest, waiting for some movement, but he remained motionless, his head bowed. Finally, without looking up or opening his eyes, he asked, "How old are you, young lady?"

"Fifteen," I said.

"Fifteen?"

"Yes, Father."

"You're fifteen years old, and you really expect me to believe that's all you've done?"

I don't expect you to believe anything, is what I later wished I had said. But I was too young to fight back. I just stood up without another word and drew the curtain aside. I couldn't wait to escape that box.

GET A GRIP!

Maura Elliot finished cleaning up the TV room and brought some dishes down to the kitchen sink. When she looked up from the soapy water, she saw that May Keane, her zany neighbor, was waving frantically to her from the kitchen window across the driveway.

May Keane lived next door with her mother Suzanne and her entire life seemed to consist of walking to CVS and back, anywhere from four to six times a day. The word on the street was that May Keane had addled her mind with drugs when she was an undergraduate, but none of the neighbors had ever asked her mother, Suzanne, directly.

Each time May Keane left the house, she sported a jaunty canary-yellow beret and a bright pink pocketbook, which she gripped tightly as if warding off assault. Maura had no idea why everyone called her May Keane and not simply May, but it may have been because sometimes when May Keane wandered off in the wrong direction, Suzanne could be heard screaming, "May Keane! May Keane!" from the doorway as if May Keane was six, not closing in on fifty.

Maura waved back to May Keane and then looked down fixedly at the dishes. When she looked up a couple of seconds later, May Keane was still waving, so she waved again half-heartedly and moved away from the window. She would finish the dishes later when not under surveillance.

Later that morning Maura stood at the side door saying goodbye to her children as they got on the bus. She had not left her house in four months. She'd been fine for a little while after Howard had deserted her, but then, one morning, when she went to the door, she found she just could not go through it. It had been the same every day since.

It was possible to remain sequestered because of grocery deliveries and her oldest son, Mike, who'd acquired his license a year earlier. Mike loved driving and never balked at carting his little sister Liz around, especially when Maura paid him so well to do it. Mike and Liz were so caught up in their own high school dramas that sometimes Maura wondered if they even realized she was housebound. They knew that their father had moved out, but they seemed to operate under the notion that if they said nothing about it, it wasn't real. Maybe they were just relieved not to be subjected to his mood swings any longer. In either case, neither one had asked her a single thing about him since the day of his departure when she had briefly explained he would be working out of the Dallas office for the next few months.

Today, she did what she'd been doing every day since her

agoraphobia had set in. She took out her endless to-do list and attacked the house. She cleaned, she mopped, she descended into the depths of the basement and sifted through fifteen years of detritus, sorting and discarding as much as she could. While she worked, she hummed along with WMJZ, the classical music station.

For ten years before she'd gotten married and had kids, she'd worked as an architect at Cole Redding. Now the only place she would allow her mind to go was into the buildings she'd designed. While she worked, in her mind she was roaming the rooftop garden and atrium at the Marygrove plant admiring the ceramic glazed bricks, the neoprene gaskets they'd used in lieu of caulk, the futuristic water towers. Other than future and past designs, she refused to contemplate anything else except the next task at hand. When she ran out of chores, she made up more—washing the walls, unearthing and polishing the never-used silver.

For the most part, this was the same way she'd operated during the late stages of her marriage. If she did not want to hear what Howard was saying, she could carry on whole conversations with him without processing a single word. It was as if someone had drilled a hole in the base of her head so that his words dripped out like water from the bottom of a flowerpot. What he was saying—that he wanted to leave, that he loved someone else, that he felt like he was "self-actualizing" and she was not—washed right through her leaving no residue at all.

Around 11 a.m., the doorbell rang. Maura heard it, but she was nearly finished with her final load of laundry. Assuming it was the UPS man, she ignored it. But then it rang again. And again. And again.

"Shit!" she muttered, tossing a pair of balled-up socks into the basket. Who could be that rude? She located her button-down sweater and put it on over her T-shirt, buttoning it up to the collar. She smoothed out some creases in her khakis and put on her loafers. Then she hurried downstairs and opened the door.

It was May Keane. She was clutching the pocketbook and peering repeatedly over her shoulder. Without acknowledging Maura, she threw open the screen door and scurried past her into the house.

"The meeting is starting," she called out, sounding frantic. "Should have started at 9 a.m. You're late! Sit down. Sit down. Wait! You better make coffee. Did you get the pastries? Hurry! Hurry! Hurry!"

Maura was alarmed, but she talked herself out of it almost immediately. After all, she had no reason to believe May Keane was dangerous. She'd lived next door to the woman for five years without incident.

"May Keane," she said. "There is no meeting going on here. I think you are mistaken. Where is your mother?"

"She went to the land of Costco, where all of her dreams come true," May Keane said, walking quickly on into the dining room. Maura followed her. In the dining room, May Keane took a seat at the table so that she was facing the wall. Maura continued around to the other side of the table to get into her line of sight.

"Would you like something to drink, May Keane?" Maura said. She needed an excuse to leave the room and call Suzanne from the kitchen.

"Yes," May Keane said, "I'd like a jasmine tea with a side of lime or cucumber, if you have it." She placed her purse on the table in front of her but kept her hands clasped tightly around it.

Maura went into the kitchen and located Suzanne's cell phone number on the list taped to the refrigerator. Suzanne answered breathlessly on the first ring, as if accustomed to emergency calls.

Suzanne sighed as Maura told her what was going on.

"Well, that's a first," she said. "Normally she doesn't like to interact with people."

This was true. May Keane had never spoken to Maura before. Sometimes she seemed to recognize Maura and the kids, and other times she hurried past them looking terrified, as if they were wild animals on the loose.

"I'm in the checkout line at Costco," Suzanne said. "I'll be there as fast as I can . . . it'll probably take me twenty minutes. I'm sorry. I know you have your hands full as it is. Just humor her."

"What do you mean?"

"It's just, in her world . . . I guess what I'm saying is . . . just go along with it . . . she has an active imagination." The answer was so disjointed that Maura was reminded of a supposition she'd made about Suzanne, whose thin hair blew this way and that in the wind, and whose outfits were always mismatched, oversized and dumpy looking. The supposition was that living with the daughter had unhinged the mother.

Maura went back into the dining room. She'd forgotten about the tea, but May Keane reached up to take it anyway.

"Thanks so much," she said, taking hold of the imaginary cup, simulating a stirring motion and then leaning down to make loud sipping noises.

"Delicious. Just right! You did it perfect!" she said.

Suddenly, her head whipped around. "You hear that?" she said. "They're here! They're here!"

Before Maura could react, May Keane backed up, scraping her chair on the wood floor.

Maura winced and followed her to the door, inadvertently catching a glimpse of herself in the hall mirror. With the rings under eyes and her black hair pulled back into a bun, she looked like a nun.

"It's a man," May Keane said. She was on her tiptoes peering through the peephole. "I think it's your guy."

"My guy?" Maura asked.

"Your guy who lives here," May Keane said.

"I don't have a guy anymore," Maura said. Howard had left her for his malnourished, bucktoothed secretary. It was a pathetic story, so cliché that when people asked what happened, she lied rather than tell them the stupid, sordid truth.

May Keane opened the door, and of course, there was no one there. But Maura's heart had done a little flip as the door swung open, and she immediately chastised herself for having any anticipation at all at the thought of seeing Howard.

"Come in, come in," May Keane said, waving an unseen person into the room. "Have a seat in the dining room. The meeting is just about to start. Isn't it great to see him!" she said, as she passed Maura on her way back to the dining room.

"Who?" Maura asked.

"Your man! Your man!" May Keane said.

"My man is not my man any longer," Maura said. "He lives in Texas."

"So, what are you doing here in Michigan?" May Keane said to the empty dining room chair where the imaginary man was presumably just taking a seat.

She cocked her head and listened for a minute. Then turned back to Maura and whispered, "Who's he talking to on that cell phone anyway? Seems to me he ought to pay more attention to the people standing right in front of him, you know?"

Maybe May Keane had picked up on Howard's cell phone addiction; maybe she had been watching her neighbors more closely than Maura had realized. If she'd known that, she definitely would have shelled out money for the expensive plantation shutters.

May Keane sat down at the dining room table and looked over at the spot where invisible Howard was sitting. Maura looked down at her watch. Fifteen minutes until Suzanne rescued her. She really wanted to get that laundry done. After that, her plan had been to finish re-grouting the basement bathroom shower stall. It had been an ambitious undertaking for one day, even without an interruption of this magnitude.

"Oh! There goes the door again!" May Keane said, popping up.

"I don't hear it," Maura said, then remembered Suzanne had warned against insisting on reality.

May Keane hurried to the door and looked through the peephole.

"Good God!" she cried, flinging the door open.

"Who's there?" Maura asked.

May Keane didn't respond. She gaped open mouthed at the door. Then she stepped aside and waved another hallucination into the room.

"Who's there?" Maura asked again.

"Stedman forgot to let the dogs out," May Keane whispered to Maura. "That's why she's late."

"Oprah?" Maura asked, stifling a short, nervous giggle.

May Keane put her arm up in midair, around what she must have believed to be a shoulder. "I watched you every day, Oprah," she said. "Every single day. Why'd you go off the air? Huh?"

When they reached the dining room, May Keane pointed to one of the empty chairs.

"Maura's man! Maura's man! Hey you! Get off that phone! Oprah's here!"

May Keane pulled out a chair. "Would you like me to get some coffee?" she said to the empty seat. She cocked her head then turned to Maura.

"She doesn't drink coffee. Do you have some peppermint tea?"

Maura nodded and headed to the kitchen. Once there, she stood next to the oven. She felt a bead of sweat trickle down her back. She thought about a church she'd read about in Belgium designed with thin sheets of steel to give the illusion of transparence. When viewed from different angles, the church disappeared completely. The architects said they were exploring the idea that not seeing something doesn't mean it isn't there. Perhaps they'd like to hear May Keane's thoughts on that.

"Doorbell!" May Keane shouted.

Maura didn't move.

"I'll get it!" May Keane called.

Finally, the thought that May Keane might actually be dangerously unstable and burst through the swinging door with a weapon propelled Maura forward.

She peeked into the foyer where May Keane was once again on tiptoes at the peephole.

"Holy Mother of God!" May Keane shouted. "It's Thomas Jefferson! Come quick! Come quick!"

Maura continued through the swinging door pretending to carry a tea set into the room.

"Thanks so much for bringing the tea." May Keane pointed to the table. "Just set it down right there."

Feeling foolish, Maura pretended to put the tray down in front of May Keane.

"Help yourselves everyone," May Keane said in a high formal voice before turning to the empty seat to her left.

"I really like those pantaloons and that cravat," she said. Then she waggled a finger at Maura. "Sit down. We can't start without you."

Maura hesitated. She wasn't sure where all the people in May Keane's mind were sitting. Finally, she chanced a chair on the far left.

"Thomas Jefferson! Holy shit," May Keane said. She nodded a couple of times as if in answer to something, then got up and moved to the chair at the end of the table.

Once there, she pounded on the table.

"Excuse me, madam," she said in a low gravelly voice. "I've been called to this gathering and have traveled a great distance to be here."

Maura glanced at her watch. Five minutes until Suzanne returned.

"Who is leading this meeting?" May Keane called out. She looked at Maura, then cocked her head again.

"Your man says he doesn't have all day," she said.

Maura grimaced as if she'd actually heard him. *Get those kids in gear! I don't have all day. Forget your hair. I don't have all day.*

"This small girl cannot be the leader of the movement," May Keane said in her Thomas Jefferson voice, pointing at Maura. Then she jumped up and moved to the Oprah chair, where she shouted back in a higher voice. "She can be the leader and she is! She is!"

Maura tried to inhale, but it felt like she was sucking through a cocktail straw.

"Your man says he hopes marriage is not on the agenda. What do you have to say to that?" Her eyes narrowed as she waited for Maura to respond.

"I am honored to have you all here," Maura said.

May Keane got back up and moved into Jefferson's seat. She banged on the table again. "As our enemies have found, we can reason like men, so now let us show them we can fight like men also." Then she bolted up and walked stiffly over to the window where she stood staring out at the empty street. She clasped her hands behind her back in a stance that really did remind Maura of an elder statesman. Maura remembered a quote she'd once read from Thomas Jefferson: "Architecture is my delight, and putting up, and pulling down, one of my favorite amusements."

"The question is," May Keane shouted, turning away from

the window, "are we going to participate in the politics of cynicism or the politics of hope?" She walked purposefully to Maura and clapped her on the back. Maura felt her heart catapult into her mouth.

May Keane strode back around to the other side of the table, sat down, and took a BIC pen out of her purse. Then she began furiously scribbling on the thick protective pad covering the mahogany dining room table. When she was done, she cleared her throat.

"I have drawn a smiley face," she said, looking at Maura.

Maura stared at her.

"Hold the applause," May Keane said. Then her mouth opened into a big *O* again. She turned to Maura.

"Your man is saying that you are fat!"

Maura said nothing. In truth, weight was the least of his complaints. He'd called her old, ugly, done in. He'd told her he was more attracted to the cat. The last time Maura had left the house was the day her friend Carol had taken her to Nordstrom to have a makeover. When the makeup artist was working on her, Maura had made what she'd thought were just a few harmless self-deprecating remarks about how much she hated her crow's feet and her neck and her jowls. Finally, the girl had put down her makeup brush and put a hand on either side of Maura's face.

"Get a grip!" she said. "You're beautiful!"

Carol had nodded in agreement. Instead of inspiring Maura, the speech had done the opposite. Every time she'd tried to leave the house since, she heard the words in her head—get a grip.

May Keane stood up and pounded on the table. "We have

real enemies in this world. These enemies must be found. They must be pursued, and they must be destroyed."

"I don't know if we need to go that far," Maura said.

"Change will not come if we wait," May Keane shouted. "We are the ones that we've been waiting for. We are the ones we seek." She walked over to the empty seat and simulated picking something up. "Let's go, Mister," she said.

Maura watched as May Keane made yanking motions. She dug her heels in and leaned back. She tried to scoot the chair out, to no avail. She looked like she was playing tug-of-war. She wiped her brow and said, "Whew!" over and over again.

In May Keane's mind, there was an enormous immovable object in the chair where Howard once sat. How many nights had Maura sat across from him, wishing him gone? How had she forgotten that?

May Keane slumped over on the floor breathing loudly, then she wiped off her hands and kicked the chair over.

"Ya! Ha!" she yelled. She took hold of the imaginary object and began dragging it backwards toward the door. If May Keane had been on TV and only her face were visible, Maura would have been convinced she was straining to lift a piano.

Maura stood up. "Let me help you with that."

TELL THEM
I'M HAPPY NOW

A week before I gave birth, the new people moved in across the street. It was mid-winter. I watched from my window. A young woman about my age, early thirties, was standing on the front lawn in a long robin's egg–blue parka. When she turned around, I noticed a baby wearing a matching blue ski cap hitched to her in a baby carrier and a toddler in a red one-piece snowsuit clinging to her leg. A third boy, maybe six, was fashioning snowballs and firing them at the stop sign. The woman waved her arms around like a crossing guard, directing the moving men here and there. I didn't see a husband anywhere.

A couple of days later, I waddled over with banana bread. I was overdue. I'd been off work for two weeks, and I was so bored I would have proffered communion wafers to the Devil if he'd turned up for a chat. Banana bread was the only thing I knew how to make besides chocolate chip cookies. That morning, I had made the chocolate chip cookie batter first—which in my estimation anyone would prefer to banana bread—but I'd eaten it all while I waited for the oven to preheat.

The woman's name was Theresa. She invited me in for coffee. She was wearing short shorts and a midriff T-shirt even though it was frigid outside. Her stomach was as flat as a plate. She had the sleek, unmarred legs of a window-display mannequin, and her thick blonde hair was parted in the middle and ran halfway down her back. Seeing her reminded me of all those years I had spent imitating Marcia Brady—wielding pom-poms while somersaulting and holding a hand up to shield my broken nose.

They'd come from Denver, Theresa said. The weather was great there, but she wasn't a big fan of the prefab subdivisions. She was glad to be here in the Midwest in a real, old-fashioned neighborhood with sidewalks and trees.

"I love old houses like this one," she said. "I'm so excited to get to work on it."

"I wish I felt the same," I said. "It tires me out just thinking about all the stuff we still have to do . . . the carpets, the kitchen, the plaster . . ."

She silenced me, swiping her hand through the air.

"Once you take the first step," she said, "it's much harder to stop than to keep a-movin'!"

She sounded just like my mother.

Theresa's house was spotless. The two older children were watching television in the family room and didn't look away from it as we passed. They were so quiet I felt like I had entered the public library. This was one of my first impressions of life with kids, and it proved misleading. The living room reminded me of something I had seen somewhere. I couldn't put my finger on it. Even the area rug in the living room—a maroon and olive Oriental—looked familiar.

"I love that rug," I said.

"Pottery Barn," she said, leading me into the kitchen. "The whole house is Pottery Barn. I left all the old crap in Denver and went on a big spree when we bought this place."

There was a beautiful floral arrangement on the mantle flanked by silver candlestick holders and family photos. The only things on the kitchen counter were a cappuccino maker and a toaster.

"I'm sorry it's such a mess," she continued. "I just feel like it's out of control sometimes. Like I can't get a handle on it."

She walked over to the cappuccino maker and turned a dial. "Do you like lattes? I can make you a decaf . . ."

"Sure."

I'd forgotten all about lattes. We were too broke for lattes.

"I'm having a double," she said. "I was up all night painting my daughter Rachel's bathroom."

The baby was sleeping in a car seat on the kitchen table. He looked fresh out of the pouch. I wasn't experienced enough with babies to guess his age, so I asked. Six weeks, she said. She said his name was Nate.

"How do you paint—with the baby?"

I had read that you should never leave a car seat or a bouncy seat on a table. I stationed myself next to Nate with one hand on the rim of his seat. "And when did you unpack?"

"I did that the first night." She handed me the latte. She'd produced a thick, peaked whip. "I can't stand boxes. Rachel's birthday is on Sunday. She really wanted a Barbie bathroom, so I figured what the heck! I'm up anyway with the baby! Why not paint?"

"Geez," I said. "It would freak me out to start a project like that."

After coffee, we went up to look at the bathroom. It looked exactly like my childhood Barbie bus—a pinkish purple hue I'd never seen on any surface since. She'd actually re-created a life-size Barbie on the wall opposite the toilet so that—somewhat disconcertingly—Barbie appeared to be staring down at the facilities.

Theresa explained that by employing a combing technique, she was able to create the illusion of wallpaper.

"I'm very impressed," I said.

"Oh, it's not done." She pointed up at the ceiling. "I missed a couple of spots up there, and I still have to install the shelves."

That night I told my husband, Ed, that our new neighbor had already managed to paint her daughter's bathroom.

"She must be on something," he said.

I climbed into bed and arranged the pillows to accommodate my large midsection.

"Nobody has that much energy," I said.

It was 9 p.m. I could barely keep my eyes open.

"She's probably painting the kitchen tonight," I added.

"I got a defective model."

I glared at him.

He grinned, and I hit him with a pillow.

I met Theresa's husband, Jim, two days later, the night before I gave birth to Christopher. We were sitting in the living room when he walked in. Theresa was drinking merlot, and I was nursing a Coke. He didn't look our way. He didn't look at the kids, who were glued to Barney. He came in on tiptoe like a thief. He probably would have continued right past us down the hall to the kitchen if Theresa hadn't brought me to his attention.

"Our new neighbor," she called out, pointing to me. He walked over, still studying the ground, then offered me his hand without looking directly at me. I noticed that he was very good-looking. In fact, he was the type of person who is so good-looking it's hard to hear what they're saying. He had black hair, short in the back but long in the front, with bangs that hung like a drop cloth over his eyes. He may have spoken, but if he did, I was too mesmerized to notice.

"Go look at the bathroom," Theresa said to him. "I'm pretty well finished. Now I'm thinking we should fix up the basement for the kids . . . you know, like a castle? Take a peek down there. Everything in miniature. You'll totally be able to see it."

In his abashed stance (he was still studying the carpet), he reminded me of that dopey actor Keanu Reeves. Finally, he brushed his bangs aside and glanced briefly at Theresa.

"Will do," he mumbled. Then he loped off toward the kitchen.

After a week of sleepless, frantic motherhood, I looked out the kitchen window one morning and burst into tears. The trees were naked. The wind was howling. The houses lining the street looked like upturned coffins. The only thing I wanted was sleep, but there were dishes in the sink and diapers on the counter. Even after I did the dishes, more appeared. It felt like I'd entered my own private horror film, an endlessly recurring nightmare. My grandmother always had dreams that there was a lion chasing her. I couldn't relate to that at all, but I would have screamed aloud if someone made a movie about dishes that materialized out of thin air or laundry that proliferated unchecked. I spent a good portion of each day breastfeeding and crying in my bed.

Then, my mother showed up.

"Let me see! Let me see my grandson!" she squealed as she burst through the door. In her hip-length mink, she resembled a linebacker.

When I held him up, she said, "What in the world is wrong with his face!"

"Infant acne," I said. "The doctor said it would clear up in a week or two."

She looked aghast.

"He gets it from me," I added.

"You never had acne!" She shook off her pelt, and I hung it up in the hall closet. "Anyway, we have a new acne clear system at Mary Kay that'll fix him right up." My mother had been Mary Kay's top beauty consultant in Pittsburgh for thirty years and was now proud to call herself a director.

"No, my hormones. Apparently, he's expelling hormones."

"Through his face?" She was fixing her hair in the mirror, lining the white-blonde ends up like scythes behind her ears.

"So I'm told."

"In that case, I'll hold off on pictures for a couple of days. Am I still sleeping in the basement?"

The next day, I had just put Christopher down for a nap and was headed upstairs to join him when the doorbell rang. It was my mother-in-law, Mrs. White. When I opened the door, her voice hit me like a slap. I fought the urge to shush her. Since Christopher's birth, our house had become her own personal toll booth—she couldn't pass by without depositing something in our kitchen, but she always made it quite clear she was on her way elsewhere.

She placed a pan on the counter and glanced at the full sink and the paper-strewn breakfast table.

"I'm headed to Neam's Market," she said. "They're having a great sale on my favorite La Crema Chardonnay."

"Great," I said.

"Just let me say hi to your mother before I go," she said, sweeping past me.

In the living room, she shrieked, "Angela!" as if greeting a salesperson at the opposite end of Macy's rather than my mother in the next room. I winced and listened for a cry from upstairs, but there was nothing.

Mrs. White was still in the living room chatting with my mother when the doorbell rang again five minutes later.

"Sheesh!" I hissed. I was never going to get my nap.

It was Theresa. She was carrying a wicker basket. I tried to thank her and shoo her out the door, but my mother yelled out, "Yoo hoo! Who's that?" and I had no choice but to lead

Theresa out to the sun porch where my mother was reclining on the chaise.

Mrs. White was sitting on the love seat opposite my mother. She sat stiffly on the edge of it with her knees pressed together and her hands in her lap. For twenty years she'd been an EMT. She had cultivated the wide-eyed, panic-stricken look of one surveying a disaster area and the drinking habits of a still-bristling survivor. When Theresa and I walked in, she popped right up.

"This is our new neighbor, Theresa Dixon," I said.

"Welcome to the neighborhood!" Mrs. White said with a bow.

"Hello!" my mother said. She closed her compact and put it back in her purse. She had just finished reapplying her lipstick—mandatory after every meal. I have never seen my mother without makeup. When I was little, I snuck into her room one time (strictly off-limits), and there was lipstick all over the pillowcase. Many years later, when I kidded her about wearing makeup to bed, she said, "I only show one face to the world."

"I brought treats," Theresa said, holding up the basket. Then she set it down on the coffee table and undid the bow to reveal homemade spaghetti sauce and gnocchi, Caesar salad, and fudge caramel brownies nestled on a red-and-white striped tablecloth. She said she'd picked the basket up at Pottery Barn.

"Sustenance!" Mrs. White announced, peering down at the booty as Theresa emptied it out onto the table.

"Thank you so much!" my mother said. "I was just getting up to cook dinner, but now I can just relax and enjoy the baby!"

"Theresa owns her own business," I said to keep myself from singing "Alleluia." My mother, if given the chance, probably would have whipped up one of her signature happy-face meals. When I was a child, she thought she could fool me into eating nutritious food by disguising it. She cut liverwurst sandwiches into the shape of bunnies and tulips. She put scoops of tuna fish in tomato boats and decorated them with a raisin smiley face. She lined up cauliflower and broccoli to resemble the forest outside the salmon man's home. The salmon man had pecan eyes and a red pepper mouth. It didn't take me long to figure out that the worse the food tasted, the more elaborate the decoration.

"Theresa's business is kind of like shabby chic," I said.

"Oh, I love shabby chic," my mother said.

"Well, I don't know if it's a business," Theresa said. "But I enjoy it. It's much less stressful than my old job."

"What did you do?" My mother zipped up her bag and placed it next to the brownies on the coffee table.

"Marketing and PR for Proctor & Gamble. I used to fly all over the place, and that's a little hard to do when you have three kids."

"Three kids!" Mrs. White said. "Good Lord!"

Just the week before, Mrs. White had announced that she would not be able to help me with babysitting when I returned to work. "I didn't enjoy it the first time around," she explained.

I had bit my tongue to keep from saying, "Gun shots, heart attacks, and domestic violence more your speed?"

Apparently, now Mrs. White felt the wine could wait. She returned to her perch on the edge of the love seat. "Take a seat," she said to Theresa, patting the cushion next to her.

"I can only stay for a minute. I've got to get back to my kitchen," Theresa said. "Did I tell you I'm painting it?"

"You're kidding," I said.

"What I want to do is paint the linoleum so that it looks like black and white tiles."

"You can do that?" Mrs. White said. "It won't come off when you're scrubbing the floor?"

"Polyurethane. I'm going to put a coat on afterward."

"On linoleum?" my mother asked.

"I saw it on HGTV," Theresa said. "Do you ever watch that?"

Mrs. White shook her head. "We don't watch television," she said.

"I don't have time," my mother said.

The phone rang.

"Excuse me," I said.

When I returned to the porch, they were glued to a talk show. The talk show host was interviewing mentally ill people who couldn't see their own image in the mirror. They didn't see the person who was actually standing there. They saw a monster.

According to these people (who were, for the most part, beautiful) what they saw in the mirror horrified them. They saw thinning hair when their hair was actually thick. They saw a unibrow when their eyebrows were perfectly etched. It got so bad for these people that they couldn't leave the house. The talk show host couldn't wrap her mind around it.

"That makes absolutely no sense," my mother said.

When a commercial came on, I said, "I have to nap. I have to get some rest while the baby is still asleep."

"Of course you do!" Mrs. White jumped up. "And I have to grab that La Crema before someone beats me to it."

Theresa put her treats back in the basket. "I'll just take these to the kitchen," she said. "And then I'm off to start painting."

The six months after Christopher's birth were the hardest of my life. I was the youngest child by eight years in my family. I'd never babysat much, and I didn't know what I was doing. I dreamed about the easy carefree days when I could read or go to the movies or even eat a meal in peace. Every single day I scrolled through scads of be-a-better-mommy sites—probably the worst thing I could have done for my mental health. In the afternoons I studied my mottled, amoeba-like stomach in the bathroom mirror.

It didn't help that my neighbor kept getting so much accomplished. After Theresa painted the kitchen floor, she redid the attic stairs to resemble Rapunzel's hair and turned a storage space in the basement into a palace, replete with miniature furniture.

"The point of this space is that adults don't even fit in this room," she said as we peered in through the small opening. "It's a safe zone for kids. Isn't that great?"

The ceiling was so low she must have painted the entire room on her knees. It looked like she had sawed the legs off all the tables and chairs. The room was so elaborately decorated—floral needlepoint rug, down throw pillows, double swags with rosettes on the windows—it might have been a display in a Junior League show house.

I started to avoid Theresa. Some of the other mothers felt the same way.

"There are only so many amazing projects I can ogle," Andrea said.

"She told me she weighs less than she did in college," Mary Ellen added. "I mean, did I ask her for that information?"

"And what about her kids? She says that if they want to take out a new toy, they put back the one they are playing with," Andrea said. "She claims they actually do it on a regular basis."

"I have never heard one peep out of those kids," Mary Ellen said. "It's weird, if you ask me."

"When she came to the door the other day, I didn't answer it," I admitted.

The winter passed. While Theresa's perfection irritated us all, she remained our go-to person in a crisis. I sought her out when anything unprecedented happened. She knew what to do when Ed spilled red wine on our new living room carpet. She gave me a beautiful hand-knotted entryway rug she wasn't using. One day, I complained about the comforter in my master bedroom, and two days later she showed up with one she had "happened upon" at Pottery Barn. It turned out to be perfect for the room. She showed Andrea how to re-grout her tub and gave me a copy of the *Household Companion* for my birthday, which shed light on many of my domestic conundrums but annoyed me all the same. She was a little like the smart girl in the class—we resented the fact that she knew all the answers, but it certainly came in handy.

In the beginning of March, I accepted an invitation to a party at her house. Ed wondered why we were going, seeing as I clearly had issues with her.

"How can we avoid it?" I asked. "We're neighbors!"

It turned into more than one party—it became a weekly neighborhood bash. She called it Margarita Night, and she began charging ten dollars per person. Her sister was in the Peace Corps in Ghana, and she had decided to raise money for the orphanage. Her sister even sent her pictures of the children, which she tacked to a large poster alongside the red donation tub.

The great thing about Margarita Night was that Ed and I could bring the baby, and then when it was time for bed, we'd take him home, pick up the TV monitor (our one extravagant purchase that year), and plug it in Theresa's kitchen. We were able to study our sleeping baby (whose window was visible across the street) while sipping margaritas and talking to grown-ups. It was a dream come true! No matter how irritating Theresa was, she was better than being stuck at home.

We were usually the last people to leave.

By May, there were twenty to thirty couples who regularly attended Margarita Night. The neighbors behind Theresa had fashioned makeshift openings in the fence so their kids could travel back and forth freely while the adults relaxed. One night, I sat next to Jim in one of the wicker chairs that Theresa had repainted earlier that week. Purple, pink, and white impatiens flooded the pots surrounding the deck. Lavender petunias dripped down from mossy planters suspended all around us. I would not have chosen to sit next to Jim as he had never been particularly friendly, but the backyard was teeming with people. I'd just put the baby to bed, and I was badly in need of a chair.

"I don't know how your wife does it!" I said.

"Humph," he grunted, looking down at his drink.

"No, seriously," I continued. "I can barely function, but I looked out my window yesterday and she's out here painting these chairs with three kids darting all around her! It's truly, truly amazing."

"It's exhausting," he said. He looked up and stared vacantly at the partygoers.

"Not for her," I said. "She never gets tired."

Theresa raced up to us. She was carrying a tray of empty margarita glasses. She was frantic. I had never seen her in such a state.

"You know," she said to Jim, "I think we should start serving more food. People drink too many of these. The chips and dip are not cutting it. Maybe we can charge more and order out from Chicken Shack from now on. The kids are hungry. Can you run to the store for me? I need more margarita mix. I need to make a Caesar salad and some corn dogs. I need some more toothpicks and another gallon of vanilla ice cream. Can you hurry?"

"I wish I knew why Jim is always so blah," I said to Ed in bed later that night.

"It's like that battery commercial." He closed his book and

put it back on the nightstand. "She's the Energizer Bunny, and he's the dud knockoff."

"It almost seems like he's depressed," I said. "If I were him, I guess I would get kind of bummed out living with such a busy bee."

"I agree." He turned out the light. "But it would be nice if one of us were a little more motivated."

"Nice!" I rolled away from him.

"I include myself in that assessment. Think about how great this place would look like if either one of us were like Theresa."

The conversation about Jim proved an omen, but it did not portend what I expected. At the time, I imagined she was neglecting him, driving him too hard. I even entertained the thought that he longed for someone (like me) who knew how to put her feet up.

"Maybe he'll get so worn out, he'll leave her," Andrea said. The thought had crossed my mind. Conjecturing about how hard it would be to live with a perfectionist made me feel so much better about the laundry overload and the dirty dishes and the moments when I whispered, "You'd better shut up!" as I closed the baby's door.

One night about a month later, I woke up to red flashing lights circling the ceiling, the static mumbling of walkie-talkies, and the sound of car doors slamming. I peeked out the window. A fire engine was parked in front of Theresa's house, an ambulance in the driveway. A few minutes later, a cruiser arrived, and two officers strode into the house. Jim came out in shorts and a T-shirt holding the baby. The other two children emerged and stood behind him watching silently. I batted Ed awake and he joined me. We remained in that window for what seemed like hours, peeking through the blinds. Finally, a stretcher emerged from the house, the sheet pulled all the way up.

"Oh my God," I whispered. "Is she dead?"

"Shit," Ed said.

"Is she dead?"

"Shit." Ed shook his head in disbelief.

The ambulance pulled away. The fire truck followed. The cruiser stayed behind. I called Andrea, because she lived directly across the street. She had watched the whole thing, too. We continued to talk and peer through the blinds until the cruiser left, followed by Jim in the minivan with the kids about twenty minutes later. I went downstairs and sat in the kitchen. I sifted through the drawers until I found an old pack of cigarettes. I stood outside the side door shaking in the cold, smoking three in a row. Afterward, I sat in the den flipping through the stations until morning. No matter how many blankets I piled on, I couldn't stop shaking.

The next morning, Andrea called when I was in the shower. She left a message on the answering machine, which I played, dripping and shivering in the hallway in my flimsy towel.

"It's about Theresa," she said. "Call me back. I know what happened."

According to Andrea, Jim had been afraid this was coming. Apparently, Theresa had had these episodes before, and he knew that the more painting, decorating, and entertaining she did, the more manic she was growing. Theresa had swallowed so many antianxiety meds and sleeping pills and painkillers (left over from the C-section) that she was dead by the time Jim had awakened in the night to pee. Jim told Andrea that she must have been stockpiling pills.

"She was sick," Andrea said. "I guess we should have guessed, but honestly, it never even occurred to me."

After I talked to Andrea, I walked back to my room and sat down on the edge of the bed. My teeth were chattering hard enough to chip a tooth, and my hands shook like someone unseen was operating my levers. I got back into bed and curled up into a ball to warm up. It took me a long time.

Often during those early years of parenting, I found myself staring at Theresa's house, wishing she was still there with me, missing her enthusiasm for life, even if, in the end, it was just a symptom of her illness. Three months after she died, Jim sold the house and moved to Atlanta. The rumor was he'd married a work colleague and was happy with his new life.

One night many years later, when I had three kids and was finally feeling fairly competent as a mother, I had a dream about Theresa. In the dream, she was sitting in a field of yellow flowers. Buttercups, maybe? She was smiling. She said, "Tell them I'm happy now."

It was the type of dream that seems real. When I woke up, I was sure I had actually been talking with her. She had been very adamant about wanting her family to know she was fine, but of course, I never called them.

HOW IT PASSED

The First Year:

Accompanying the pregnancy: bloating and the gentle chidings from older women in grocery aisles. "I wouldn't eat that ice cream, sweetheart. It'll take you a year to work it off."

A year? What a laugh! We've never needed to watch our weight.

After the baby, we spend endless days reminiscing about sleep and the free time we used to squander. Remember reading the *New York Times* cover to cover? Spending the whole weekend on the couch? Dancing until 3 a.m.? Sleeping until noon? Remember when we could just get up and go? To the movies? To pick up Chinese? To grab a gallon of milk?

We form a playgroup to combat the dawning realization that this is no temporary matter. The playgroup affords a forum to talk about the people we used to be. The people we'll be after we're done here. The babies zone out in their bouncy chairs, alternately crying or cooing or nodding off while we guzzle coffee and try to avoid eating too many donut holes.

It's hard because the donut holes are the best thing going.

We talk about the husbands. The husbands are not suffering enough. We picture them heaving a collective sigh of relief as they drive off down the road every morning.

The husbands complain about how hard they work, how ornery their boss is, how many deals they've sealed. The pressure is on. They need a drink. They NEED the remote control. They offer to help with the diapers but often botch the job. They don't hear the baby, or they do hear the baby, but they want to watch one more inning before they get up to get him. They spoon food into the baby's mouth, but they forget the burp rag or the bib. They rinse the dishes, but they leave them in the sink. How hard is it to load a dishwasher? They put their dirty clothes in a nice neat pile by the side of the bed. Why bother with the nice neat pile if the clothes are still on the floor?

They are useless, we decide. Before long we are peeling them apart like string cheese with our ragged, misshapen nails.

Morgan doesn't want to have sex with Cheryl. Ever.

Steve wants sex. Steve has all sorts of wacky, off-beat fantasies: Sex in the 125-year-old oak tree behind the garage? Sex in the bathroom at the Tap Room with the door unlocked?

Margery is so put off by some of the bizarre positions Steve points to in his book (of course he has a book!) that she sleeps downstairs in the study in front of the TV.

Zane is moody and unpredictable according to Tina. She's been walking on eggshells ever since his father died. She would sympathize with him if he hadn't complained so much about his father when he was alive.

Shelly is a teacher and her husband Bob is a reporter at the *Detroit Free Press*. They are broke and probably always will be. Most of their college-educated friends consider these first homes "starter homes," but Shelly knows her three-bedroom ranch is the Alpha and the Omega. She and Bob were both only children, and the one thing they agree on unequivocally is they want to have a passel of kids, no matter the cost.

The husbands might benefit from getting to know each other since we have nothing in common with them anymore. Several couples, an offshoot of the playgroup, form what we refer to as the Dinner Club. We want to see these husbands in the flesh, these men about whom we know every intimate detail.

Year Two:

Playgroup disbands. Too many babies crawling and running and knocking things over. One mother who routinely brings her coughing, hacking baby to the meetings. She always claims not to have noticed the runny nose before it starts dripping all over the coffee table.

"What's this?" she'll say, incredulous, scurrying to wipe it up.

We are so incensed we can hardly control ourselves. Why bother driving across town for organic food when we are surrounded by people who are bent on sabotaging our children's health?

Another death knell for playgroup: Cheryl's husband, Morgan, is cheating on her. We've read about infidelity, but we can't believe it's happening on our street. Cheryl's husband moves in with the new girlfriend. We bring Cheryl casseroles and commiserate with her, but privately we chalk it up to her atrocious beef pineapple stew, her lackluster sense of humor. Each of us decides (though no one says it) that if we were married to Cheryl, we would have run out on her, too. And then right after that we feel like jerks. Why are we such jerks?

Year Four:

We have more babies. No more naptime for mom. One baby bellowing all morning. Another ramming into walls all afternoon. This constant racket is getting to us. We yell and scream and cuss and then we gather at the park for mass absolution.

"Honey, I do the exact same thing!" we say. "I'm losing my mind!"

We don't know what day it is; we can't remember how to spell. What's that word? What's that thing? You know that thing you put around the baby's neck when he's eating? What is that thing called?

We crawl into bed at 8 p.m. We go back to the park. The awful bone-numbing park. *Swing, swing, swing.* We don't want to hear, "Mommy, can you push me?" ever again. We sit on benches drinking coffee. We plan the next Dinner Club; we talk about the last one. Did anyone notice how much Zane drank last month? Can you believe Tina is smoking? She's pregnant! Is that a vestige of her West Virginia upbringing? And what is Margery wearing around her neck? A portable ionizer? She's gone off the deep end, hasn't she? Did you hear the latest? She has some sort of vaginal dysfunction. She says it's painful when they . . . you know . . .

Home again.

Then the looooonnnnngggggeessssssst hooooooooouuuuuu-rrrrrrrrrssssssss: 4 to 7 p.m. The hours when the babies have made everyone cranky. Afternoons that make us feel like slugs crossing the desert.

We pour our first glass of wine at 5 p.m.

Year Six:

Suddenly, Margery is obsessed with recycling. All the problems in the world stem from our disregard for waste. Don't we know that we are polluting the planet and poisoning our children? We ought to be ashamed! We ought to be looking out for the welfare of our descendants. We ought to be protecting the world unto the seventh generation! Margery forms an environmental group, and soon she's uncovered a cancer cluster. Babies born without limbs. The air is so noxious it would be folly to attempt a trip to the park.

It is just the excuse we have been looking for.

We all think some good sex would bring Margery back to earth, and Tina gets drunk enough to suggest Margery indulge her husband in his oak tree fantasy. That's the last we see of them for three months. Ultimately, they come back to us, because what else do they have to do?

Year Eight:

Zane is drinking. A lot. Sometimes he staggers into the Dinner Club and sits mumbling on the couch in front of the fire. Occasionally someone will sit down beside him. Most often it's Margery. She's still trying to avoid frolicking in the trees with Steve. She thinks she's uncovered the reason for all of the assorted ailments, the general malaise engulfing the neighborhood:

"They used to spray the trees," she says, "with a toxin."

"I never spray my trees," Steve calls out, and Shelly, who happens to be passing with a tray of hors d'oeuvres, says, *At least not with pesticide*, and everyone bursts out laughing.

Late at night, Zane puts in a Bob Dylan CD and mumbles, swaying in the corner. The rest of us are assembled around the fireplace on various couches and overstuffed chairs. Margery is kneeling next to the fireplace trying to light the fire. When she gets up, she staggers into Zane and he grabs her arm. Then he reaches out and pinches her rear end.

"Oh, Zane! Stop!" she says. And it's the way she says it that causes everyone to pause.

Still, we aren't sure exactly what we're witnessing until Tina screams.

Year Ten:

The children are in school every morning. Margery sets up a small shop called Running Interference in the village. The store is chock-full of all-natural, nontoxic household products. People have started avoiding her on the street and in the grocery store because she's always spouting dire predictions about our health and the environment. But we stand by her. We trek to Running Interference for aromatherapy lotions and soy candles. We have our homes inspected by Healthy Homes to the tune of $200. We have our asbestos remediated.

But then the Myers girl, a first grader at Mellon Elementary, dies after what her mother thought was just a stomach flu. A rotavirus has taken her out.

No way to run interference.

For one brief sunlit week we are kissing and coddling and hugging our children. We tiptoe into the nursery at night and stroke our babies' cheeks. *Thank God for you! I don't know what I'd do without you! Why have I been so blind?* We trek to the park (we haven't been there in a year), and for that brief, gleaming week when the Myers girl is buried and mourned and the world morphs into a shiftless, unpredictable place, we push the swing, loving every minute.

Shelly and Bob have their fourth child. They have four small children under the age of ten. No one mentioned that when you decide to have four children—*bam, bam, bam, bam*—it will sound like a hammer in your head for years to come.

Shelly hires a babysitter even though she and Bob are watching their pennies. Actually, *Bob* is watching their pennies. He's inputting their expenditures into Quicken. Even toilet paper is categorized. Shelly starts hitting the "cash back" button when she's checking out at the grocery store. She has to be able to pay for a babysitter without Bob running interference. The neighbor girl, Claudia, a young girl of sixteen, initially says she's available from 4 p.m. to 6 p.m., but when Shelly gets home on the first afternoon, Claudia tells her, "I can't do this. I can't do this ever again." This validates and at the same time completely devastates Shelly, who knew this child-rearing thing was hard but not *that* hard. She would like to hit the girl, but instead she shrugs and watches Claudia flounce out the door in her miniskirt and combat boots.

Just you wait, she thinks.

Year Twelve:

Life is getting easier because three of Shelly's children are in school. The Dinner Club is not meeting on a monthly basis anymore but still manages to get together three or four times a year. Life is so busy! Sports, Cub Scouts, Brownies, business trips. Tina is trying to adjust to year-round hockey, which Zane has insisted on even though their two boys are so small they can barely hold themselves upright in their hockey gear. She doesn't even seem to notice that Zane is falling apart. Last month, he passed out before dinner, then, later in the evening, when we were indulging in the apple crisp, he ambled into the dining room.

"Well, that was delicious, Margery!" he said, before drifting out the front door and into the frigid night.

No one says anything to Tina because Tina won't respond. She's talking nonstop at the other end of the table.

"Mikey loves hockey. The parents are great. But seriously? All weekend, every weekend? I can't keep up with it."

Right, right, right. She'll talk so long and so rapidly that any hope of bringing up Zane's drinking problem dies out like the candles on the table. Zane doesn't come back. Luckily, he makes it home and into the house that night. He's been found in the yard before—sometimes in the front yard and sometimes in the shed out back. That night, the Nygards pass him on their way home from the country club and they give him a lift.

Margery and Steve are seeing a therapist. It doesn't seem to be working.

Year Thirteen:

Margery confides that she's looking for an apartment in the Village. Then one night, Bob and Steve attend a men's ecumenical retreat at the stadium. Eight thousand men swaying and praising God. Bob is already religious. (His faith and a daily dose of Zoloft are how he's dealing with his wife's spending habits—and his attraction to Emit Hughes that seemed to pop up out of nowhere one day in the sauna when Emit shifted and his towel fell off.)

Steve is not religious. But when they begin singing "Amazing Grace" and end with "Lord of the Dance," Steve feels a bright white light like a laser beam pierce his forehead. He's falling backward. When he comes to, all the jungle sex fantasies are gone, remediated.

He's been saved.

One night, Shelly and Bob are sitting in the living room. He's working on Quicken and she's reading *Oprah* magazine.

"Don't you think it's funny that none of us are divorced yet?" she asks. "You know, what about Tina and Zane? How can she put up with the drinking? Those poor kids! Margery and Steve? It's like he doesn't even exist. She's so caught up with the environmental movement. I mean, can you see what—if anything—is holding them together?"

Bob doesn't hear her. The grocery budget is out of whack. "Why don't you just buy generic?" he says.

"Good idea," Shelly says.

Year Fourteen:

Zane spends thirty days in rehab. And when he comes back, he signs on as manager of their middle son's hockey team, which means traveling every other weekend to places like Lansing and Kalamazoo. Tina has gone back to school to become a dental hygienist. Nobody knows how or why she's come up with this plan. It's such a random choice, and she really doesn't need the money.

"I mean why not pet grooming or flower arranging or even working here?" Margery asks Shelly when they are sitting in Starbucks one morning.

"I thought she was an English major," Shelly says.

"No, I was the English major," Margery says. "She was something else."

When Margery goes to the bathroom, Shelly sneaks a packet of Sweet'N Low into her coffee. Stirring the white powder makes her feel as devious as a teenager smoking dope behind the garage.

"Did Tina ever work?" Shelly asks when Margery returns.

Now that all the kids are in school, Shelly is helping out at Running Interference a couple of days a week and the two of them often take a power walk and then stop at Starbucks before opening the shop for the day. It's getting hard to keep the weight off even though they barely eat anything.

"I don't know. . . . I don't even know what you used to do. What did you do with that English major?"

Margery shrugs. "Hard to remember that far back."

Year Fifteen:

Steve and Margery pick up their son at TCBY after the eighth-grade mixer, and he's drunk. At the Dinner Club we all shake our heads.

"He threw up for four hours straight," Margery says.

"He's just a baby," Steve says. "He looked like a little wasted baby."

Margery tuts.

Zane says, "It doesn't mean he's destined for a dissolute life. You know the people who have the worst problems are the ones who don't get sick, who never get hungover. I mean, this will probably keep him off it . . . for a while at least."

Zane is back from a third round of rehab. Tina is cautiously optimistic.

"I'll be done with school in June," she says. "And then I start three days a week at Dr. Biel's office. I'll take great care of you guys. I won't gouge your gums, I promise."

"Good," Margery says. "I hate it when they take the floss to your gums like a saw. I'm bleeding all over my bib by the time they're done."

"I would never do that," Tina says. "I actually heard about this woman who flossed so violently that bacteria seeped into all the cuts in her mouth and ate her brain."

"That's crazy," Shelly says.

We decide to play charades, and since we're at Shelly's house, she invites her oldest three kids to join us. They are thirteen, eleven, and eight, and suddenly they seem to comprehend the rules. Their attention spans are longer now. They are kind of fun. It's a revelation.

On the way home, Tina and Zane and Margery and Steve all talk about the children and the possibility of including them at future dinner parties. They add something that's been sucked out of the group over the years, and whatever it is, we all feel the sparkle, a hint of renewed enthusiasm.

Year Sixteen:

Zane falls off the wagon. He passes out in the tool shed in the backyard on a frigid night, which would have been de rigueur for him if it wasn't twenty below.

"Why rum?" we all ask later when we hear about the empty bottle of rum found beside him. Zane had always loved his manhattans.

Perhaps there was an old bottle in the basement or maybe in the back of a kitchen cupboard. Perhaps it was hidden behind the flour and Tina forgot to pour it down the toilet. We won't ask her. Not now. Not that she was ever capable of answering questions about Zane.

Tina is surrounded by people.

We drop off casseroles and coffee cakes.

Tina asks Steve to speak at the funeral. Steve doesn't want to; he didn't even like Zane, not really, but how can he say no?

Writing the eulogy, he conjures up some vague images of Zane swaying to Bob Dylan.

He jots down *music*.

There were a few quiet mornings together up north pheasant hunting.

"Hunting," he notes.

They shared a modicum of respect for Richard Nixon's foreign policy initiatives, but he's not going to talk about that.

"Hockey," he writes. "Long-time hockey manager."

The kiss. He hasn't thought about the kiss in years.

"Pinched my wife," he writes, then crosses it out.

What can he say about Zane?

"Zane was like that picture of Dorian Gray," he writes. "Zane was that guy who lived high up on the hill. The one everyone was jealous of; the one no one knew. . . . What was the name of that story?"

When the rest of us think about Zane, we see him swaying and mumbling along with Bob Dylan. We remember other evenings with the Dinner Club, but we can't recall any insightful moments or any time when Zane revealed himself to us. In all these years, there has not been one aha moment when Zane really came alive for us.

Steve is at his desk for hours—well into the night—trying to come up with something meaningful. Zane's kids went to the private school and his went to public. Zane had two kids. Did he ever talk about them? Did Zane ever talk about his job? What did he do? Some sort of corporate lawyer.

Successful. Wealthy.

Steve makes a list of these attributes. It's quite substantial.

There's nothing to be ashamed of here, he thinks. But it's not a lot of insight for fifteen years of friendship.

The church is full.

"Who are all these people?" we ask each other at the funeral.

Margery says some are from the office, some are from church.

Shelly is filled with sadness. Not for Zane so much. For herself.

If she died tomorrow, what would these people have to say about her? She looks over at Margery, who is weeping. She looks down at the little cloth-covered box in the aisle. All that is left of Zane.

Margery hiccups softly. Shelly wonders what happened between them. Was that a lone pinch or was there more to it? How sad if that was just a smidgen of what had passed between them. The possibility exists, Shelly suddenly realizes, that Margery meant more to Zane than Tina did.

The possibility exists that Margery was the love of his life. The possibility exists that Margery didn't know Zane either. Maybe his wife didn't know him. Or his kids. Maybe nobody in the entire church knew Zane. Shelly rubs Margery's arm, and she hopes that someone—she doesn't even care if it is Margery—knew him well enough to mourn him deeply.

Otherwise, it's all been such a waste of time.

Margery unfurls her Kleenex and blows her nose. The music starts.

There's a flutist, and the music drifts toward us in the back row where we are sitting. We are hiding. We don't want to talk to anyone. We tell ourselves that we want to be free to express our pain during the eulogy. We tell ourselves we are crying for Zane, but deep down we know the truth.

WHERE'S THE BABY?

Sharon didn't answer when she felt the first vibration in her jeweler's apron, or even the second one, but when she pulled out the phone and saw it was her older sister, Evie, calling for the third time, she put her brass brush down on the table.

"I'm teaching," she whispered, trying not to put any inflection on the word teaching. She shouldn't have to give a reason for ignoring her sister, who up until this illness had never offered any excuse herself.

"Have you heard about the baby?" Evie asked. It sounded like she was crying.

Sharon could hear a car going by in the background on the other end of the line. She had turned away from her class to take the call, so she turned back to smile at the seven middle-aged women in her jewelry making class. They were all in the final stages of creation, sanding off the sprues and brushing down the metal, and they appeared to be ignoring the phone call, though Plump Nora at table one had started humming, a sure sign she was listening.

"Where are you?" Evie was not supposed to be driving.

Sharon had hidden her keys in the cookie jar before she left for class.

"The street signs say Broadmoor and Thrush? It's spelled t-h-r-u-s-h." Evie sounded it out like a child.

"How did you find the keys?" Sharon said. Evie loved cookies. It had been a stupid idea to hide the keys in the cookie jar. "Can you make it home?" Sharon asked, although the answer seemed obvious.

"I think so?"

"OK. Stay put. I'll be right there. Just wait for me."

"But what about the baby? There's a dead baby here. Should I call someone?"

"A dead baby?"

Plump Nora stopped humming and looked up at Sharon. A couple of the other women also appeared startled. Sharon shook her head and put her hand over the phone.

"Not a real baby." She tapped the cell phone against her forehead. "My sister is not well."

Plump Nora nodded sympathetically, which for some reason irritated Sharon. She turned away from them again.

They were the same seven women who always took her class—the same ones who never finished any of their projects. Every class, Plump Nora brought donuts, and every class, all her skinny, suburban classmates demurred and stared as Plump Nora devoured half the box. If her sister had been in the class, she would have made a snide comment about Nora being a Dunkin' Donuts poster child.

Sharon had often wondered whether Evie reserved her rude remarks for family members or if she had berated people all over the country when she was touring with her band. Evie was seventy-two, fifteen years older than Sharon, and Sharon had never spent more than a weekend with her before her Alzheimer's diagnosis. Sharon had no way of knowing for sure, but her guess was everyone who met Evie got a little dollop of mean. Joe, the drummer in Evie's Double Time Jazz band, had almost dropped out after she'd called him a tone-deaf asshole. She'd been calling him an asshole for thirty years, but it was the tone-deaf part that'd pushed him over the edge.

Sharon held her finger up to let her class know she was almost done with the call.

"Where is the baby exactly?"

"On the sidewalk in front of this rundown, old house."

"OK. Well, stay away from it. Get in your car and lock the door. Don't move. I'll be right there."

"Don't move, or get in the car?"

Sharon had hoped the progression of the disease would be gradual, but Evie's symptoms had accelerated markedly over the last two months. There was no way she should be driving. Ever.

Sharon sighed. "Get in the car, lock the door, then stay put."

Sharon followed the computerized voice of Mitzy, her navigator, toward the city. Tyler, her son, had programmed Mitzy to sound British eight years ago when the Dodge Caravan was new, around the time he'd transitioned out of the neighborhood public school to the Ridgeton School twenty miles away.

Evie's band had broken up when the saxophonist, Gary, was diagnosed with pancreatic cancer five years earlier. Gary, Evie, and Joe had been the core of the jazz band, fixtures in

New Orleans. Joe lived in the same apartment building as Evie. He was the first one to notice that after Gary died, Evie was spending whole days in her apartment watching *Lost* reruns and subsisting on Planters peanuts.

One day it dawned on him that she was watching the same episode over and over. He took her to the doctor, where she failed a series of aptitude tests. Sharon flew down to New Orleans the following week and was shocked by the state of Evie's apartment—shoes in the dryer, Honey Bunches of Oats cereal in the cat bowl. She suggested a move back to Michigan and was caught off guard when Evie agreed.

It felt a lot longer than two months ago.

Since Evie had moved into the apartment over Sharon's garage, she'd yelled at a young girl at the mall for using the water fountain (disgusting/unsanitary/vile) and at a woman using hand weights on the treadmill at the gym (do you want to break your fucking neck?).

And then there were all of these far-fetched notions—delusions really. The current one had to do with whether people Evie encountered on the street, in the pharmacy, at the doctor's office, had "paid the cover," a question she'd taken to shouting at random intervals. At least this one was based in reality—a vestige of Evie's years playing in New Orleans, where she'd made a living off tip jar donations and cover charges.

Sharon turned down Thrush Road and passed a team of parolees in orange vests picking up trash. Detroit was enjoying a comeback, but only in Midtown so far, and Evie had ended up in a terrible part of the city. On the next block, a single, abandoned house remained amid the prairie grass.

As she drove, she felt her resentment escalating. It felt like she was being saddled with a deranged interloper. She'd rarely heard from Evie over the years. When she'd gotten married in 1992, Evie had sent a Snoopy Christmas card with Merry Christmas crossed out and "Happy Wedding" scrawled above it. In 1994 for Tyler's birth, she'd sent another card with a generic "Congratulations on the birth of your baby" with no reference to Tyler's name or any indication that she'd bothered to learn the gender of the baby. In 2002 when their mother died, Evie had flown into Detroit for the funeral.

Still, even then, in the funeral home with their mother's open casket in front of her, Evie had been her usual callous self, leaning over to whisper, "What is up with your son?"

"It's called autism," Sharon had said.

"It's like a record skipping. He just keeps asking the same question: *When are we going? When are we going? When are we going?* I don't know how you can stand it."

How ironic Evie's observation seemed to Sharon now.

Sharon parked behind Evie's Volvo and dialed her sister's cell. She didn't want to get out of the car so close to the parolees—not that they were desperate for women in late middle age, but still.

"Hello?" Evie asked, as if she had no idea who it could be.

"It's me. I just pulled up right behind you."

Sharon watched as Evie turned her head around as slowly as a swing bridge someone was cranking by hand.

Sharon waved to her.

"Mom?" Evie asked, waving back.

"It's your sister, Sharon."

"Oh," Evie said, sounding relieved.

Why would she confuse Sharon with their mother? She looked nothing like their mother, who was svelte like Evie, not short and stocky. Secondly, their mother had been a raging alcoholic, as volatile and unpredictable as the cast-iron gas burner in Sharon's jewelry studio.

Sharon prided herself on complete control of her emotions and her alcoholic intake—no more than two glasses of wine per night. Their mother had been inebriated for so long and so relentlessly, that by the time their father finally defected with his French Canadian office manager, no one could blame him.

When Sharon was a teenager, Evie had never missed a chance to tell her that their mother had gotten pregnant with Sharon so late in the game as a last-ditch attempt to save her doomed marriage.

As if her mother hadn't already made that very clear.

Evie still didn't move. Sharon got out of the car and hurried over. She leaned into the driver's side window. "I will come back for your car. Grab your purse."

"Absolutely," Evie said, reaching for her purse. "But what about the baby? It's right over there." She pointed outside the passenger side window.

Sharon looked over at the sidewalk.

The parolees were almost upon them, making their way up the right side of the road collecting trash with their long-handled grabbers. The sidewalks were an inch deep with detritus because the city had started shutting off services, forcing people to move downtown so that they could further shut off services to the outlying neighborhoods. Sharon scanned the weeds: a black trash bag, a Chiquita banana box, a striped hobo bag, a large box stuffed with newspapers, a dead houseplant. No baby, of course.

"What did I tell you? You don't see that every day," Evie said pointing.

"Evie, it's just trash."

"I bet it's *the* baby." Evie marched over to the trash pile.

Sharon could just envision Evie crawling on the ground. She hurried after her and put a hand on Evie's arm.

"Here's what I'll do. I'll call 9-1-1 on the way home. There's nothing else to be done if the baby is dead."

"Is that what the world has come to? Mothers dumping babies on the sidewalk?" Evie asked as Sharon took her arm and steered her toward the car.

"It is a crying shame." Sharon bit her lip to keep from adding something snide about Evie's lifelong disdain for children. Once, during Sharon and Phil's rough patch, Sharon had told Evie she'd hired a babysitter so she and Phil could rekindle the flame. They were both so burned out by Tyler (God love him) that Pastor Rich had pronounced the vacation crucial.

"I don't get it. Why do you need a babysitter for an eighteen-year-old?" Evie had said. "Is he really that slow?"

It had taken Sharon a long time to get over that comment. Was she even over it now? Despite the fact that the principal at Ridgeton was "sure" that Tyler would "optimize his full potential" if they paid $35,000 a year in tuition, it turned out they had wildly different calculations about his potential.

•

When they were sitting down to dinner that night, Sharon told Phil she'd had another incident with Evie.

"Can't say I'm surprised." Phil passed her a container of curry noodles and unpacked his own pad thai. One of the things Sharon loved about Phil was that he relished the routine of Meatloaf Monday, Thai Thursday, and Stew Sunday as much as she did.

The phone rang. Phil set his chopsticks down and got up to answer it.

"Hello, Pastor!" he bellowed into the phone.

Phil always greeted Pastor Rich with the enthusiasm most people reserve for long-lost relatives. Pastor Rich had been Phil's BFF ever since he'd steered them through their marital quagmire. His advice had centered on acknowledging the different languages of love—Sharon's "acts of service," Phil's "physical touch," and of course Tyler's language, which wasn't in the book but which Pastor Rich called "ask and ye shall receive."

If Phil wanted Tyler to express affection, he had to ask for it directly. Phil was supposed to say, "I'm feeling like I need a hug." He was not supposed to let it bother him that Tyler couldn't comprehend why.

The fact that her son shied away from physical touch had never bothered Sharon all that much. She had never been touchy-feely either. She could remember only three times when her own mother had ever hugged her: once when she broke her leg bicycling in second grade, once in seventh grade when she'd tripped over a tangle of Christmas lights and banged her head on the corner of the piano, and the day she graduated from high school—then simply because the photographer had trained his camera on them.

"Your sister called Pastor Rich this afternoon," Phil said when he returned to the table.

"She said she was going up to take a nap. How did she even get his number? She must have done it when I went back in the cab to get her car." Sharon dumped more pad thai on her plate.

"Apparently, she wanted to talk about the baby."

"I was just going to tell you about that." Sharon set down the carton.

"Have you told him about the dementia?" Phil brought his chopsticks to his mouth.

"It hasn't come up."

"She told him the baby was on the sidewalk, so he got in his car and drove down there to check. Poor guy. I filled him in. He's got the picture now."

The following week, Sharon received another call. The Grand Ridge Police Department had Evie in custody. The police officer, a blond man with a thin mustache, told her that her sister had been picked up walking along the highway. When they'd asked her what she was doing, she'd said, "I'm going to get the baby."

"The dead baby?" Sharon asked.

"She didn't mention a dead baby. She said something about an abandoned baby."

"Abandoned?"

Sharon told him about Evie's diagnosis. "Last week it was a dead baby," she said.

On the way to the station, Sharon tried to keep from

crying. She was not going to let this bring her down. She'd withstood the disappointment of autism and a nonexistent relationship with her mother. But seriously, how much more could she take? She took a deep breath. Probably, a lot more. People withstood a lot more. She had to look on the bright side. Phil could be annoying, but he was a bright side. The jewelry making could be a bright side, if she ever got the chance to pursue it. Tyler's autism was not a bright side, but at least he was functioning, holding down a job.

When Phil walked in the door, Sharon asked him to sit down in the living room for a minute. He said he wanted to change. He was going fishing; the steelhead had just started running.

"Five minutes is all I need. I've come up with a game plan. Here's the gist of it—I feel guilty, but I also feel like my sister should not be my problem. I don't feel anything for her. Like nothing at all. I know that sounds terrible . . ."

Phil shrugged. "Understandable." He went over to the closet. "Let me just get my tackle box out and then we can talk."

Sharon followed him and stood by the bifold doors. "I want some time for myself. Is that too much to ask of the world? After what we've gone through with Tyler . . . Frankly, I mean, I don't think I have it in me to be a caretaker again."

"So, what do you want to do? Put her in a home?" Phil retrieved his fishing vest.

"Yes."

He pulled his tackle box out of the closet. Studied it as if it had the answer. "I don't think that sounds unreasonable given the circumstances. If we can find one that's not too expensive."

"I keep wondering why I'm even hesitating. She couldn't have raised one child. She's never done one thing for me. She left me alone with the worst mother on the planet, and then when I did see her, she'd say things like, 'Sharon, you ought to try this diet. Sharon, what's with those dowdy dresses? Sharon, that looks like lipstick a clown would wear.'"

Phil laughed.

"It's not funny! You try listening to it for a lifetime and let me know how funny it is then."

When Sharon went up to the apartment the next day to bring Evie's groceries, she found Evie dressed in a black flapper-style dress and bright pink galoshes with a line of lipstick running across each cheek like Indian war paint. A sterling silver necklace with rose appliques Sharon had made for Evie last Christmas was broken and dangling from the coffee table in the foyer. Sharon picked it up and put it in her pocket. She should have known Evie wouldn't appreciate it. In the tiny living room/kitchen there was a half-eaten piece of chocolate cake sitting on the leather ottoman, crumbs all over the floor.

"What in the world are you thinking with all that makeup and those galoshes?" Sharon asked as she steered Evie toward the bathroom.

"It's not my fault." Evie pulled away from Sharon. "I know you blame me, but it's not my fault."

"No problem. I know it's not your fault."

"This party is for musicians, and children aren't allowed, so you are going to have to leave."

"I'll be on my way then." Sharon tried not to sound as exasperated as she felt.

"Are you drunk, Mom?"

"Not yet," Sharon said.

When they reached the bathroom, Evie put her hands up on either side of the doorjamb and refused to enter.

"You better not keep it."

Sharon let go of Evie's shoulders. "Keep it?"

"That kid."

"What do you think I should do?"

"I don't know, but you can't handle it."

After she finally got Evie settled in front of the television, Sharon went out front to adjust the sprinklers. Across the street, three little boys were chasing each other and screaming.

Sharon wondered if it were possible that Evie had tried to talk their mother into giving her up or even aborting. She'd been fourteen years old when their mother was pregnant with her. Old enough to understand their mother's limitations. One time when she was ten, she had to call Evie in New Orleans because their mother was passed out on the sofa in the living room. She'd vomited all over a stack of *Good Housekeeping* magazines. Evie had suggested she go to the neighbor's house next door. The Whitneys were nice, she said, and they wouldn't mind.

"They moved last year," Sharon had said.

"Too bad, I practically lived there when I was in high school. Well, put a blanket over her and turn her on her side. She'll come to eventually."

After that, afraid of what she might find, Sharon had stopped coming home after school. Instead, she often went to the library or her best friend Molly Jacobson's house. The summer after junior year, the YMCA offered a discounted jewelry making class that ran on weekdays from 1 to 5 p.m. Sharon signed right up. She spent her summer mornings in the library, her afternoons at the jewelry making class, and her evenings at friends' houses—anything to avoid interacting with the woman she'd taken to calling *The Creature*.

"Hand your pain to Jesus," Pastor Rich would have said if she'd confided in him about the sadness that felt like heaps of refuse collecting in her chest.

As if Jesus were the garbage man.

Later that evening, Tyler called from his computer repair job where he worked three nights a week. It was better for him to work at night when no one was around because interacting with people was a strain, but some nights there was nothing to do at the shop, and then he called incessantly.

Sharon told him she'd spent the day with Aunt Evie.

"It's sad, Mom," Tyler said. He'd witnessed Evie's outburst at the mall, when she'd yelled at a girl for using the water fountain.

"I know it."

"Is she a pain in the butt?" One time a teacher at the public school had called Tyler "a pain in the butt," and he'd never forgotten it.

Though she would have liked to answer truthfully, Sharon said, "No, she isn't."

"Nobody's perfect," he said, which is what he said every time she got mad at him for blowing the leaves into the driveway instead of onto the tarp or shoveling snow back onto the driveway.

"You've got that right," Sharon said.

Sharon did some research and located an assisted living center five miles away that was both inexpensive and well-regarded. Look at all the fun activities, she would tell Evie. Great food! And best of all, Monday night is Music Monday! Maybe Evie could perform for the other residents.

When Sharon went up to Evie's apartment the next morning, she found Evie sitting in the kitchen staring vacantly at the news. She was eating peaches straight out of the can.

Sharon said she had something to tell her, and Evie shushed her.

"Wait until my show ends," Evie said.

Sharon took a seat at the kitchen table and scrolled through Facebook on her phone. It was incredible how much time Pastor Rich wasted posting quotes he considered inspirational, which were so often inane: *God knows the journey you need to take before you do,* and *I'm blessed and I thank God every day for everything that happens to me.* Give me a fucking break, Sharon thought. She wanted to reach into the phone and pinch Pastor Rich. Hard.

She shut the phone off. Evie was watching the news as if the newscaster were Billy Graham offering her the keys to the kingdom.

The feel-good news story at the end of the broadcast was

about a woman who had lost her four-year-old daughter in New York. The doors closed between them on the subway. Luckily, a Good Samaritan had stayed with the girl on the platform until her mother was able to ride the subway back to pick her up. It turned out the girl didn't even know her last name or her address.

"Isn't that a wake-up call for all parents?" the newscaster asked his sidekick, a blonde in a bright green top.

Evie turned to Sharon. "I found the baby," she said. She lifted another spoonful of peaches to her mouth.

Sharon glanced over at her. Evie had painted one of her eyebrows on very dark. "What baby?"

"I don't even know why selfish people have babies in the first place," Evie said.

"Where is this baby?"

"In the back seat of the car!" Evie shouted. She put down the peaches, got up from her chair, and hurried out of the room.

Sharon followed her down the stairs. Evie flung open the door and shielded her eyes from the glare of the sun.

"Where's Mr. Whitney?" she said.

"Who?"

"Mr. Whitney! Mr. Whitney!" Evie pointed to the house next door.

"Our old neighbor? Why in the world do you want him?"

"He has her." Evie stomped her foot.

"Who?"

"The baby!"

"Why would he have the baby?"

"You were passed out. You left her in the car!"

"What are you talking about?"

"Mr. Whitney has to save her." Evie turned to Sharon. "This isn't my job!" she said. "I can't save your baby!"

Evie turned and went back up the stairs to the apartment. Sharon followed.

"What are you talking about?" Sharon said. "Did Mom leave a baby in the car? Am I the baby?"

When Sharon tapped her on the shoulder, Evie turned around and asked if Sharon had seen her guitar.

"It's probably in the closet," Sharon said.

In a minute, she'd forget she was looking for her guitar, and she'd start looking for yogurt or her hairbrush or maybe even the dead baby again.

Watching her, Sharon felt a sudden pity. She had not been the only one to live through the debacle that was their mother. What if her mother had left a baby in the car? What if Sharon had almost died? What if Mr. Whitney had saved her? How terrifying would that have been for Evie?

"Well, all of that happened a long time ago. We aren't in danger anymore," Sharon said out loud, even though she knew Evie had probably already lost the thread of the conversation. Maybe somewhere deep in her subconscious, Evie would be comforted.

"You don't know that," Evie said. She plopped down on the couch and pressed her fingertips into her temples.

Sharon sat down next to her. She couldn't remember the last time she'd hugged her sister. If ever. She put an arm around her shoulder.

Evie looked over at her, startled. "Did you pay the cover?" she asked.

"You bet I did," Sharon said.

THE PHANTOM ARM

Mark Grantham woke up one morning to find that he had grown a third arm. He was seventeen years old. He'd stayed up late studying the night before, and at first, he thought the arm was an extension of the panic attack he'd suffered right before he'd turned out the light. He was going to fail his Chem test on Monday. Then he'd never get into college, and his arch nemesis, Gilbert Lagrasso, would secure valedictorian. Forget Harvard or even the University of Michigan. He was going to end up at some community college or worse—trade school. He'd rot in his parents' basement forever, eating Cheetos, watching reruns of *The Walking Dead,* and fending off baffling texts from his mother:

mt dshwr pls
fd snk

He went to the bathroom and splashed water on his face, and that's when he noticed the third arm. It was more like a hologram of a third arm. He could see the wall through it. When he moved over to the full-length mirror on the back of the door, he saw that it was a forearm growing out of his own left arm just below the elbow. As he stood looking at himself, it went straight up like a crossing guard's arm. Then it waved.

Mark found his mother in the kitchen standing next to the sink staring at a countertop littered with dirty dishes. He tapped her on the shoulder. When she turned toward him, she didn't flinch or look startled or even glance at the arm. *She couldn't see it.*

"I know this is going to sound strange, Mom," he said, "but I have this . . ."

"Would you look at this mess?" she interrupted, sweeping her hand across the room.

His sister Tricia had left the side door wide open all night and dishes piled in the sink. On the couch, his mother had discovered an overturned bowl of Froot Loops. Buster, the terrier, had gotten into the Froot Loops, then puked on the carpet. She'd stepped in the mess and ruined her slippers.

"It looks like a poltergeist blew through here!" she yelled. Mark glanced around the room.

"God only knows what time she got in!" His mother shook her head. She walked over to the kitchen table and plunked down into a chair.

Tricia was a year younger, but in every possible way she was beyond Mark, except, of course, in grades and test scores, accomplishments that only endeared him to people over forty.

"I'm sorry, Mom. I'll help you clean this up, but I have a big problem." Mark took a big breath.

"First, I have to tiptoe around her because her boyfriend's broken up with her and she's fragile. Didn't I tell her that nice girls wear pants?" His mother put a hand up to her cheek and scratched it absentmindedly.

Clearly, she was already losing her shit. What would happen if he told her about the third arm?

Mark returned to his room and got into bed. Luckily it was Sunday. Maybe if he went back to sleep the third arm would just disappear. He closed his eyes.

An hour later, Tricia knocked and then peeked in.

"You busy?" she asked, and then, without waiting for a reply, she ran over and jumped onto his bed. "What the hell happened to me last night? I have no fucking clue!"

Before Mark could respond, the palm of the third hand turned face up, as if to say, *Do tell.*

"Big night?" Mark asked.

"It wasn't supposed to be a rager. I went to this party at Jessica's house. It started out low-key. Maybe I had one too many shots of watermelon vodka? God, I feel like crap!"

She rubbed her forehead as if she was trying to scour off the pain. There was a slight lime tint to her skin, but she still could have walked the runway. Mark had been on acne meds so long that his neighbor Angela Anderson was a top salesperson for the product. His story was the main part of her spiel: *My neighbor, Mark, looked like a leper. If there was ever a kid you could've called pizza face, etc., etc.* Then she would show people his before and after pictures. In this way, she made a killing.

"The last thing I remember is standing on the couch yelling, 'Am I right, ladies?'"

"Right about what?"

"That's what I want to know!" Tricia laughed. "I have absolutely no clue!"

"Tricia!" their mother called up the stairs. "Where the heck are you?"

"Shit," Tricia whispered, ducking down behind the bed. "Don't tell her I'm here."

"Hey," she whispered a moment later. "Guess who's down here under the bed?"

"Who?" Mark asked, and for a second he was terror-stricken. Maybe there was more going awry than just his arm.

"Buster!" Tricia whispered.

Buster had been hiding for the past week since he had been attacked by the pit bull who lived next door. Tricia and Mark had nicknamed him the "Assassin."

"Poor Buster," Tricia said. "Come on out, buddy."

Buster whimpered, but he wouldn't budge.

When Mark woke up on Monday, the third arm was still there. He decided he would just go to school and behave like nothing was wrong until he could figure out how to handle the situation. Since no one else could see it, there was no way the arm could interfere with his day-to-day life, and possibly, if he ignored it, it would simply disappear.

Besides, he was sure it was psychosomatic. In AP Psychology he'd read about every crazy disorder under the sun. After people had limbs amputated, they often felt and even saw a phantom arm. This was nothing unusual. It was some kind of stress response. Besides, if it was something worse, he didn't want to find out before the SATs on Saturday.

The first person Mark encountered upon leaving the house that morning was Mr. Pastan, the owner of the Assassin.

Rumor had it, Mr. Pastan had escaped from some frightful-sounding town in Siberia. He always wore a black pea coat like a spy, even in the summer, and carried a long-handled poop grabber out in front of him like a blind man's walking stick. He marched his pit bull, the Assassin, around the neighborhood at 8 a.m., 11 a.m., 3 p.m., 6 p.m., and 10 p.m. like clockwork. Whenever Mr. Pastan issued a command, the dog would stop in its tracks.

"Mr. Pastan and the Assassin," Tricia said. "It's got a nice ring to it."

The Assassin had taken a chunk out of Buster the week before because someone (probably Tricia) had left the gate open. The day of the attack was the only time Mr. Pastan had ever talked to Mark in all the fifteen years they'd been neighbors. He'd pointed a finger at him and yelled: "Keep that dog in yard. Next time I not save it!"

Despite Mark's animosity toward Mr. Pastan (and the Assassin), as soon as he spotted Mr. Pastan that Monday morning, his third arm started waving enthusiastically, as if they were best friends. Mark wondered if the arm was just being sarcastic like his father who always yelled, "Have a great day!" whenever people honked at him.

In school, Mark rested his real arms on his desk, and the third arm rose up from his elbow and waved to Mr. (dead) Enders in History and Mrs. (snot) Rotherman in Calculus. When he was carrying his lunch tray, it stuck out at an odd angle and waved to the popular kids with their band T-shirts and sandals. It waved to the kids who were too basic for words.

All through English, while the teacher, Mrs. Campbell, discussed Annie Dillard's *An American Childhood*, the hand remained quiet, but then toward the end of class it made some finger motions as if it wanted to make a point. Mark took out his phone and googled sign language.

He didn't hear the bell. When he looked up, everyone was gone, and Mrs. Campbell was standing next to the door staring at him.

Mark smiled at her and got up. "Sorry, I'm stressed out. I have a Chem test."

Mrs. Campbell didn't return the smile. "Mark, I'm surprised you had nothing to say about Dillard's work. How about: 'Knowing you are alive is watching on every side your generation's short time falling away'? Doesn't that just get you right here?" She pointed to her heart.

Poor Mrs. Campbell. Everyone called her *the ancient ruin.*

"It kills me," he said, trying not to crack up as his third hand put its fingers together and played a tiny violin.

Gilbert Lagrasso caught up with Mark in the hall. The only thing Gilbert (6′6″, size 13 EE shoes, oily black curls) had going for him was his GPA. His glasses were thick, and his lips were as red as if he'd just finished munching on a cherry lollipop.

"Did you study for Chem?" Gilbert asked.

"A little."

"I am totally going to bomb this one." Gilbert shook his head, but the curls remained shellacked to his forehead.

"You always say that."

"I know, but this time it's true."

"Say, Gilbert, do you know sign language?"

Mark knew that Gilbert spent most of every weekend glued to Rosetta Stone, because a couple of years back Mark had decided that since they were the smartest kids in the class, they ought to hang out. Also, he had decided this because he had no other friends. Unfortunately, it was soon clear that Gilbert didn't have time for friends. He was too busy learning new languages. At last count, he was up to ten, including Latvian and Esperanto.

"Of course I know sign language," Gilbert said. "Why?"

"Someone was trying to speak to me the other day. He kept doing this." Mark held up his right hand and made the sign his third hand was making.

"That doesn't mean anything." Gilbert looked puzzled.

"Really?"

"Really. You're just doing some weird mishmash with your fingers. That's not a word. Here let me show you." Gilbert put his books down on the ground and proceeded to demonstrate the entire sign language alphabet.

"Hm," Mark said.

"You really didn't study?" Gilbert picked his books back up.

"I didn't study. I'm probably going to fail. And you know what? I don't give a shit!"

Several people turned away from their lockers to stare. He'd said it louder than he'd intended.

"Lovers' quarrel?" Tim Meisel, the football quarterback asked, and the hall erupted with laughter.

Mark glanced over and saw that Tricia was at her locker. She slammed it shut and pointed a finger at Tim. "Shut your face, Meisel."

Tim put both hands up in surrender and several kids laughed.

Gilbert slunk off toward Chem, and Mark followed him.

The Chem test, and Chemistry in general, was the only thing standing between Mark and a 4.3 GPA. A 4.3, plus being editor of *The Tower,* a Rotary Club scholarship recipient, a Meals On Wheels volunteer, a member of junior varsity track, and a level five pianist, might just make him Harvard material. Maybe.

The first section of the test went really well, but then halfway through, Mark looked up to see the third hand making bunny ears on the wall.

He had his yearly checkup with his pediatrician, Dr. Howell, the next day after school. When the nurse called his name, he asked his mother to remain in the waiting room while he went in to see the doctor.

"With pleasure," she said, returning to her *Real Simple* magazine.

Dr. Howell had been his doctor for his entire life. He was a big man with meaty arms who spent most of Mark's exams talking about the Lions, Tigers, or Red Wings depending on the season. It was a one-sided conversation because Mark knew nothing about sports. His father had taken him to a few Tigers games when he was little, but he'd been so bored that the vast discrepancy between what he was experiencing (tedium) and what his father was feeling (pure bliss/glee) was truly disturbing.

"So, how is everything, Mark?" Dr. Howell set his laptop down on the counter and turned it on. "Still top of the class?"

"I think so, sir. Well, it's between me and this other guy."

"A fight to the death!" Dr. Howell laughed. "If I were a betting man, I'd put my money on you."

"Thanks."

When Dr. Howell approached him to begin the examination, Mark put his arm in his lap so that the third arm was flush against his chest. Later, when Dr. Howell palpated Mark's stomach, his hand went right through the ghost arm. Mark tried not to wince. It didn't hurt, but for some reason he felt sorry for the arm. In general, why couldn't adults be more considerate of his personal space?

"Anything wrong?" Dr. Howell asked. "You seem a little tense today."

"SATs are Saturday. I had a Chem test today. Lots of pressure junior year."

"What do you have to worry about? Sky's the limit for you!" Dr. Howell picked up his laptop and headed toward the door.

"Dr. Howell? I have a quick question," Mark said, stepping down from the examination table.

Dr. Howell paused, his hand on the doorknob. "Yes?"

"I'm doing this project for AP Psych and I was assigned this totally bizarre case." Mark paused. There was absolutely no way to say it without sounding ludicrous. "You know what? Forget it. I'll ask my sister's psychologist."

"I didn't know Tricia was seeing someone?" Dr. Howell raised his eyebrows.

"Oh, sure. She goes out all the time, she doesn't try in school, she just broke up with her boyfriend. My parents think she's a total disaster."

"Typical teenager."

"Yeah."

"You set the bar pretty high. Poor girl doesn't stand a chance."

Mark tried to study for the SATs but ended up watching six episodes of *The Walking Dead* instead. The hand snapped its fingers in delight every time a zombie went down. When Mark woke up the next morning, he was so tired he was tempted to tell his mother he was sick. He'd never missed a day of school. He and Gilbert were the only ones out of the 1,600 students at his high school who could say that.

In the hall on the way to class, the hand shot up and waved to people Mark had never spoken to in his life: Cindy Williams, the head cheerleader, and Ray Kirby, the star baseball player. It pointed its finger at Andrea, who'd once called Mark a turd, and Britt, who'd proclaimed him "dweeb-like in every dimension." By the time he got to Chemistry, Mark was following the arm's lead. If it said "hi" to someone, he did too. If it waved, Mark waved his real hand. To his surprise, a couple of people actually smiled back. One of the popular girls even said, "Hey, Mark."

Mark couldn't believe she knew his name.

In Chemistry, Mr. Boyle walked over to him with his test and put it down on the desk with a thwack. "C+."

The hand gave an enthusiastic thumbs up, so Mark gave an actual thumbs up, and the class burst out laughing.

"You think this grade is funny?" Mr. Boyle asked.

"A little bit," Mark said.

"How so, Mark?" Mr. Boyle leaned in.

"You wouldn't understand."

Someone in the back of the class snorted. Mr. Boyle frowned down at him.

"Try me."

"I'm sorry, Mr. Boyle," Mark said finally. "I don't think it's funny, but . . . I finally decided I can't let the pressure get to me. It's not healthy."

Mr. Boyle blinked. "Really? That's quite mature, Mark. I don't appreciate the laughter, and I don't think you're doing yourself any favors with this grade, but I agree with you in principle." Mr. Boyle looked around the room. "Maybe the rest of you should learn a thing or two about sangfroid from Mark here."

Gilbert caught up to Mark in the hall after class. "Sangfroid? What the hell is up with you?"

Mark shrugged. He had been thinking about the $3,342 he had saved from his lawn mowing jobs. Maybe, instead of going to college, he would drive across the country, camp in Yellowstone for a month. Maybe he'd end up like that kid who starved to death in the bus in Alaska, but maybe not. Maybe someday he could work in his cousin Nick's fly-fishing shop out in Montana.

"Man, you're totally screwed with that grade!" Gilbert said.

"Try not to sound so happy," Mark said.

Gilbert followed him into Calculus and sat down next to him. "Just tell Boyle you had a death in the family or your mom is sick. Something. Make up some excuse. You're so close! Save yourself!"

Mark's mother was sitting at the kitchen table in her bathrobe when he got home from school. It looked like she hadn't showered or combed her hair. Normally she had tennis or gardening club or was working at the library. He'd never seen her in her bathrobe at 3 p.m. before. She had baked chocolate chip cookies, his favorite. When she saw him, she got up and moved listlessly toward the fridge for the milk. Had she sensed the arm? Had she picked up on his distress? She poured him a glass of milk and sat back down across from him.

Mark picked up a cookie. It was still warm. He bit into it. "These are awesome, Mom." The hand gave her a thumbs up.

"Thanks," she said without smiling.

Mark was just about to ask her what was up when Tricia blew through the back door, dumped her backpack on the floor, kicked off her combat boots, and passed through the room without so much as a glance their way.

"No screens!" his mother called after her. "Do your homework!"

"Whatever," Tricia said. She clomped up the stairs.

Her bedroom door slammed. Mark crammed the rest of the cookie into his mouth and picked up another one. The hand did a little finger roll, excited about a second treat.

Luckily it wasn't attached to his right hand or it would have belted him in the face while he was trying to eat. The thought made Mark giggle, and his mother stared at him.

"What?" she asked.

"Nothing."

She shook her head and filled her cheeks with air, puffing them out like a chipmunk. Then she blew it out slowly, making a prolonged whooshing sound. "I guess it's just the SAT tomorrow," she said. "I know how worried you must be! I just want you to take it easy. I just want you to know that we love you and we're behind you."

Mark's father called him into the living room that evening for a chat. Tricia was sitting on the couch scrolling through messages on her phone.

"So." His father set the paper aside. "Tomorrow's the big day?"

"I'll be fine," Mark said.

"I hate to say it matters . . ." his father said. He shook his head and took a swig of his Heineken.

"So dramatic, Dad," Tricia said. She reached into the bowl of candies on the side table, unwrapped a chocolate kiss, and popped it in her mouth. "Is Mark going to spontaneously combust if he doesn't get a perfect score?"

"I wish you worried more, young lady."

"Unlike you, I'd like to keep my hair."

The third hand made as if to chuck his dad on the cheek with a friendly "buck up," so Mark reached out with his real hand and did it. "Lighten up, Dad! It's just a test."

His father stared at him. "I thought you'd be freaking out."

"I was just thinking I might take a gap year," Mark said.

"A what?" Tricia asked.

"A year off from school just to roam around."

His father started laughing. "You? I'd like to see that!"

"I think I'm going to do that too," Tricia said. She peeled the wrapper off a miniature peanut butter cup and bit into it. "Can I come with you, Mark?"

"Sure," Mark said.

His father licked his thumb and turned the page of his paper. "Stop eating all that candy, Tricia. Mark, you ought to get a good night's sleep tonight. You need to be well rested for the test."

"I do what I want," Tricia said, just as Mark said, "Sure, Dad."

"You are such a kiss ass," Tricia said to Mark. She stuck her tongue out at him.

"Watch your mouth," Mark's father said.

"Watch your mouth," Tricia mimicked silently behind his back. The hand thought that was hilarious. It snapped its fingers in appreciation.

Mark was heading toward the stairs to study when Tricia pointed to the front window. "Look, it's Mr. Pastan and the Assassin!"

"Now, now, that's no way to talk," his father said from behind his newspaper curtain.

"That guy is such a jerk," Tricia turned to Mark. "He

doesn't even care that his stupid dog traumatized Buster. Poor thing's still under my bed! I wish we could do something."

"Maybe we can," Mark said.

"Ha ha!" Tricia said. "I'm in! What are we going to do?"

"Don't you kids say one word to him." His father put his paper down and looked at them sternly.

Mark walked over to the front door, Tricia behind him. "I didn't think you had it in you," she whispered.

Mark flung open the front door.

"Oh, Mr. Pastan!" he shouted.

Mr. Pastan stopped in his tracks and stared up at him. Mark stared back. Behind him, he could hear Tricia giggling. "What are you going to say?" she asked. "What are you going to do?"

Mark continued down the front walk toward Mr. Pastan, Tricia trailing behind him.

"You know, Mr. Pastan, your dog cannot go around biting other dogs."

Behind him, Tricia said, "That's right."

"Now it's payback time," Mark continued. "As my father likes to say, 'When you least expect it, expect it.'"

Mr. Pastan stared at Mark stone-faced for what seemed like an eon. Then he let go of the Assassin's leash.

"Oh shit," Tricia said.

Mark heard the sound of Tricia's feet and the screen door slam behind him, but he didn't turn around. For several seconds, Mark and the Assassin eyed each other. When the dog didn't move, Mark finally glanced over at Mr. Pastan. Mr. Pastan was looking down at the Assassin in disbelief. Mark took a step backward toward the house keeping his eye on the dog.

Mark took another step backward and the Assassin's ears went up. Mark froze. But then the Assassin turned his head. He appeared to be homing in on something Mark couldn't see down the road. What was it? A rabbit? A squirrel? Mark took another step backward while the Assassin wasn't looking. He had almost reached his front steps.

"Come on, come on, come on," Tricia whispered to him from the door. "Run for it."

Mark was just about to turn and make a break for it when the Assassin barked and raced down the sidewalk toward the intersection, his leash dragging on the ground behind him.

From the doorway, Tricia started hooting. "Go, go, go!" she yelled.

Mr. Pastan shouted a word that sounded like "Bark!" in a language that might or might not have been Russian.

When it was clear the Assassin was not going to stop, Mr. Pastan stormed off after him like a soldier charging into battle, his long-handled pooper scooper extended in front of him.

"He's gone, Mr. Pastan!" Mark called after him. "He's free!"

THE VISIT

Summer 1976

My mother and father decided I could use a companion, so they invited a distant cousin to come stay with us over the summer. Although I wanted to spend my summer reading in my fort (alone, if possible), I knew better than to share that preference with them.

"Who is she?" I asked.

"My cousin Tom's daughter. She's eleven, like you," my mother said, smiling with teeth.

"Terrific." I smiled back, trying to mirror her expression. Smiling with teeth was non-negotiable for my mother. I had been taught to offer up my smile like a slice of cake to everyone I met.

This cousin arrived two days later, on a plane from Grand Rapids, Michigan. My mother had grown up outside of Grand Rapids, but I had never been there. One time when I asked her why we never went back, she dismissed the question by quoting some famous guy. "You can't go back and change the beginning, but you can start where you are and change the ending."

Cousin Tom was the only relative still living near my mother's childhood farm. Her parents had both died when my mother was in high school, so she had little reason to go back. Cousin Tom had never traveled to Washington, D.C., or anywhere else, according to my mother, and I had never met or even heard of his daughter before.

When I learned that her name was Janice, I pictured a heavy-set girl with braces, glasses, and possibly a limp, but the girl who appeared in the gateway at the airport was three inches taller than me and looked like she weighed half as much. She had long black hair and light blue eyes and wore a comb in the back of her Guess jeans like all the cool girls in my class.

"Hello!" my mother said, smiling with teeth and throwing her arms around her.

"Hello," Janice said to us, no teeth.

"Oh dear," my mother said as we hauled Janice's giant green suitcase off the carousel. "How am I going to fit this in the Mercedes?"

Once the bag had been hoisted into the trunk and we were all settled, my mother looked back at us in the rearview mirror and asked Janice if she had enjoyed her flight.

"It was fine," Janice said. She sat with her hands clasped in her lap, looking out the window.

My mother's mouth twitched. "Well, I just want you to know we are so happy to have you this summer. You and Marie are going to have so much fun. Have you ever been here before, Janice?"

"No," Janice said, "I've never been anywhere." She said this with exasperation in her voice, the same tone I sometimes imagined using when my mother chastised me. *What about this knife, Marie? You cleaned the whole kitchen very nicely, but you left this knife here on the counter. Is that the way we do things?*

"You are in for a treat, Janice! This is the big city!" my mother continued. "I moved here when I was twenty-two. I had never been out of Michigan until then, so you've got me beat!"

We dragged the suitcase up the stairs to my room and heaved it onto the other twin bed. What could this girl possibly have stuffed inside it? I only owned three pairs of pants, three pairs of gym shorts, three T-shirts, and three dresses for church. I had one pair of sneakers and one pair of dress shoes. My mother didn't like clutter. Clutter is what led to Grandma Jean's problem, she said.

"You keep piling up and piling up and one day you'll find you can't even get through the front door." This was true of junk that attached to your body as well as junk that filled up your home.

My mother had suggested I show Janice around the neighborhood, but when I asked her if she wanted to go outside, she said, "I really need a nap."

If I were a guest in a stranger's house, I would have shadowed the host even into a tar pit. But Janice seemed to keep her own counsel, an option I had never considered.

After I left Janice in the bedroom for her nap, I found

Gert in the kitchen doing dishes. Gert was from Jamaica, and she'd been with our family since I was six weeks old. When any of my classmates asked me what Gert did in our house all day long, I said she was my nanny.

"She's not your nanny," my mother always corrected me. "She's the housekeeper. You don't need a nanny because your mother is not working. Remember that. I gave up my job to take care of you." My mother had been a secretary before she had me, but my father was a successful lobbyist, so she no longer had to work. She said she had quit working to care for me, but I saw so little of her with the garden club and tennis club and who knows what, that she might as well have been off somewhere running a Fortune 500 company.

My mother liked Gert to wear gray uniforms with white piping, so she had purchased three of these getups and hung them in the hall closet. Every Tuesday morning, Gert arrived in the passenger seat of a light blue Chevrolet Nova from some undisclosed location, hung her jeans and T-shirt in the closet, and changed into one of the three uniforms. During the week she lived in the third-floor bedroom, and every Sunday morning she hung her dress back up, changed into her street clothes, and left for her two-day break.

If anyone had ever asked me, I would have said that Gert was the person I could not live without. After school, Gert and I enjoyed tea and toast while watching *The Brady Bunch*. On Saturday nights when my parents were enjoying date night, we watched *The Love Boat* and *Fantasy Island*. On Wednesdays and Fridays, when Gert did the laundry, I sat in an old, tattered armchair next to the dryer and read. Gert was the person who walked me to school on the first day of first grade. And Gert was the person who sat next to me all night in the hospital when I needed an IV to combat dehydration induced by the stomach flu. My parents were in Europe at the time.

I told Gert that Janice was in my room taking a nap.

"You be nice to her," she said. "You know she got to be sad since her mommy left."

This was something my mother had not mentioned, but I didn't dare let on or Gert would have clammed up. My mother had once castigated Gert for informing me that there are people in the world who don't believe in Jesus.

"I know," I said, "but she could make an effort." According to my mother, any outcome could be put to right if one made an effort.

Gert clanged a cup down on the yellow Formica counter.

"Listen here, little Missy. There's trouble in this world you know nothing about. Don't go telling that girl how she should or shouldn't behave until you've lost your own mother in a hot minute." Gert shook her head and made the clicking sound with her tongue.

When Janice emerged two hours later, she was wearing a frilly white shirt with her Guess jeans. She said she was ready to go outside.

"Do you want to see my fort?" I said.

"Your fort?" She looked at me like I had just crawled out of a garbage can. I wasn't sure if she was disgusted by my suggestion or my clothing. I looked down at my cutoff jeans and dingy gray T-shirt and was suddenly ashamed. Up until that moment, I had been in the habit of trying to ignore my appearance, even though my mother had told me on more than one occasion that dresses were the best option for people like me who have a "great future behind us."

Janice and I walked across the street.

"You have to crawl through the chain-link fence," I said.

"I think I can handle that," Janice said.

She was so skinny she made it through the hole without snagging her frilly shirt or getting it dirty on the ground. Inside the fence there was a yellow sign indicating the forest was now a construction site. My father had told me someone wanted to build forty houses in the woods. The neighborhood was fighting it, but I had seen men wandering the woods taking pictures and measuring, so it was pretty clear the construction was moving forward. It made me sad to think that my fort would be demolished and there was nothing I could do about it. My neighbor Cassie and I had built the fort about a hundred yards down a footpath. We'd constructed it as a lean-to beneath the hollow of a honeysuckle bush, so it had smelled heavenly since April.

Inside, we kept an old paint tarp from Cassie's father's workroom along with a long stick that served as a broom and two tree stumps for chairs. Cassie was a year older than me, and over the past year, she'd stopped coming to the fort in favor of tennis practice. She had set her sights on Wimbledon and spent all her time hitting tennis balls against the wall behind the public library.

My favorite thing was to bake chocolate chip cookies and bring them out to the fort with a book and a pillow. I'd rest the pillow against a tree stump and stretch out on the tarp. Before Janice arrived, I had spent most of the summer in this way, except for the days when it rained and I had to read in bed. I preferred the fort because I loved it and I loved to read, but also because seeing me at home "lounging around doing nothing" irritated my mother, and she was apt to find chores for me if she caught me in the act.

"Yuck," Janice said, when I'd swept and laid out the tarp. "You sit on this old thing? What about the bugs?"

"They don't bother me," I said.

"Well, they bother me." She made another face, frosting on top of her routine disgust.

"So, you don't want to stay?"

She shook her head.

"OK. Let's walk down to the 48th Street Park instead." I folded the tarp back up.

"So what do you like to do back home?" I asked when we were back on the street. In the front yard of the Andersons' house, cute Michael Anderson was cutting the grass. He stopped mid-row, turned off the lawn mower, ran a dingy gray rag across his forehead, and called out, "Hi Marie." I was surprised he remembered my name. When I waved, I half expected glitter to shoot out from my fingertips. Then I realized he was looking at Janice, not me. Janice did not even seem to notice that we were interacting with the god of 48th Street.

"Mostly I just hang out with my friends," she replied. "Or go to the mall." We walked on in silence. I glanced back once and saw that Michael Anderson had resumed mowing.

My mother would not approve of Janice at all, I realized, and it wouldn't be long before she let Janice know.

"If you smile the whole world smiles with you, but if you cry, you cry alone," was my mother's favorite saying. My mother made all of her pronouncements with such authority.

It never dawned on me that she could be wrong about anything. She believed that her father had made the choice to turn to alcohol instead of the Lord. And her mother had given into food rather than fueling herself with God's love.

"When life gets you down," she said, "you pray for guidance. You march right into the battle armed with the Lord."

That night at dinner, Janice sat at the end of the table opposite my father. My mother and I sat in our usual spots on either side of him.

"Let's pray," my mother said.

Janice looked over at me, eyes wide, as my mother held her hands out. Everyone grabbed hands except for Janice, who ignored us. She kept her own hands folded in her lap and stared down at her plate. When my mother realized that Janice was not going to participate, she frowned, then bowed her head again and said grace with a little more force than usual.

After dinner was served, my father slapped his hands on the table and looked at Janice and me as if we'd won the lottery.

"We are going to have so much fun this summer!" he said, then he rang the little bell in front of his placemat.

Gert came back through the kitchen door.

"Do we have any hot bread, Gert?" he rubbed his thumb and middle finger together as if he could almost feel the bread materializing.

My mother gave him a look. "You know what the doctor said, Ron."

"Hot bread, Gert?" My father repeated.

Gert went back into the kitchen.

"So Janice, how was your first day in the nation's capital?" my father asked.

Janice shrugged a shoulder. "Good, I guess."

"What did you do?" My father turned to me as if he were expecting me to say that I had led a parade.

"Not much," I said. If Janice wasn't going to talk, I didn't see why I had to.

"Well," my mother said. "Let's talk about what we're going to do from now on."

Gert came back through the door with a round sterling silver dinner roll holder and set it down in front of my father. He took off the cover. Inside, there were four Pepperidge Farm dinner rolls, piping hot. My mother gave Gert what Gert referred to as "the ice eyes."

"I knew you'd come through for me, Gert," my father said.

He popped one in his mouth and sat chewing while my mother, Janice, and I stared at him. "I have a plan," he said when he'd swallowed it. "On Friday I'd like to take you guys to the Air and Space Museum. Would you like that?"

Janice shrugged.

"That sounds great," I said to save Janice from my mother's glare.

"You are so lucky!" my father announced. "You are going to be one of the first visitors! It just opened last week!"

"Good for you, Janice!" my mother exclaimed.

Janice stared at her.

"Can you pass the peas?" my father asked me.

"Janice, when I was your age, I lived on John Street about

three blocks from you. I'm sure your father has shown you the house?" My mother waited, but Janice didn't look up or respond.

"The only excitement there is the library and the church, am I right?" my mother asked. "Well, you are in for a good time now! And when you get back, you'll have so many stories to tell your friends about your time in the big city."

"Can't wait," Janice mumbled into her peas.

My mother had made a terrible mealtime arrangement with Gert. Every night, she made the dinner and Gert did the dishes. My father and I had suggested Gert make dinners instead, but my mother wouldn't allow it because Gert fried her food, sometimes even using butter, and this reminded my mother of Grandma Jean. Gert had told me that she would have preferred to cook so that she could head upstairs and rest her weary bones instead of waiting for us to finish. I still wonder if she ever said that directly to my mother. It is unfortunately quite probable that my mother never gave Gert's weary bones a single thought.

One time, Gert had told me about a dreadful trip down South she'd taken in the late '60s with her former employers. They were headed for Florida, and they'd stopped at a diner in Georgia for lunch, but the owners of the diner wouldn't let Gert in.

"I knew they weren't going to let me in that place," she said, with a shrug. "I don't know what they were thinking."

I thought she was going to say something more, but she just stopped speaking and picked up the laundry basket.

"If I had been there," I said, "I would have hit the owner of that diner over the head with a bat."

"Oh, that wasn't the part that bothered me," Gert said. "It was the fact that my employers went in anyway. I had to wait for them in the car, and then afterward they never even acknowledged it. They even had the nerve to bring me back a sandwich."

That night at dinner, I looked over at Janice pushing her food around and wondered what she thought of my mother's plain boiled chicken, brownish peas, and the small red potatoes with a sprinkle of dill. I should have informed her that our golden retriever, Jackson, would be waiting by my feet for dinner. To avoid starvation, I had taken to stealing Pop-Tarts from Safeway and stockpiling my classmates' lunchtime desserts—Ho Hos, Twinkies, and Oreos—in a pillow I kept in the back of my walk-in closet. Kids who were allowed sweets seemed to be able to take them or leave them.

On Friday morning, my mother dropped Janice and me off at the Air and Space Museum, where my father was waiting out front. He had walked over from his office to meet us.

"Janice, you are in for an extraordinary experience," he said, clapping Janice on the back. "President Ford just cut the ribbon yesterday! When you go back home you can tell your friends that you were one of the first people to see this new installation!"

"Cool," Janice said, wincing from the clap.

I could not have been more thrilled. I had a secret ambition to be an astronaut myself, though I had told no one.

The notion of a girl astronaut was ludicrous, and I knew it, but it was hard to keep my cool as we wandered through the hangar-like museum. If Janice hadn't been there, I would have matched my father's enthusiasm and then some.

"Look!" my father said. "The *Wright Flyer*!"

The 1903 *Wright Flyer*, the world's first airplane, looked like it might crash right into us based on the angle it had been suspended from the cables above our heads, and we stood for a long time underneath it, taking it in.

After that, we peered inside John Glenn's Mercury capsule, *Friendship 7*, and the Apollo 11 Command Module, *Columbia*, that had carried humans back to Earth from our first journey to the Moon. My father and I could barely contain ourselves, but Janice seemed to be dragging herself along like a sack of sand.

"Charles Lindbergh's plane!" My father shouted at one point, waving us over to the *Spirit of St. Louis*.

"Geez," Janice muttered. "You'd think Charles Lindbergh was still in it."

The next morning Janice said, "Does your mother serve that same breakfast every single day?" She meant the bran cereal, side of bananas, and milk.

"Yes," I said.

"I'm starving," Janice said. "I can't eat that again. I have some money with me. Can we walk to the store?"

We got dressed, pretended to eat our gross breakfasts, and then set out for the Safeway and Pop-Tarts. It was a beautiful summer morning, already steaming hot, the heat of the pavement pressing through our flip-flops.

"Why does your mother get dressed up every day like she's going to work?" Janice asked.

My mother always looked ready for a photo shoot. "She likes to be ready for anything," I said, which was the best explanation I could come up with.

"It's so far from normal," Janice said.

"What about your dad?" I figured that if my mother was such a showboat, her cousin might be, too.

"Are you kidding?" Janice said. "He's like *Night of the Living Dead*."

I had no idea what she meant by that, so I said nothing for a minute. "I think my mother just wants to do her best," I said. "If you try hard, you can do anything."

Janice clicked her teeth; a slightly different sounding *click* than Gert's, though conveying an equal measure of irritation. "That's a good one," she said.

Just before we turned the corner to Safeway, we ran into Cassie, who was coming back from the library. She had a tennis bag looped over her shoulder and wore an all-white tennis skirt and a matching top, as if she were already a Wimbledon champion and not a skinny kid hitting by herself against the library wall. Cassie's father was stationed in Africa somewhere doing who knew what (she claimed he was a spy), and her mother spent most of her time slinking around their backyard garden yanking things out of the ground, so Cassie was on her own most of the time just like me.

"Hey, what's up?" Cassie asked when she reached us. I could tell by the look on her face that she was surprised I had landed a new friend. I had no friends in my class, mostly because I said all the mean things I wanted to say to my mother to other people instead, people who had no power over me. These things slid out of my mouth without warning like slugs. Things like: "Do you really think that looks good on you?" or "You know I don't think you were meant to be a singer." Afterward, when the person looked at me horrified or hurt or a little bit of both, I always felt like the worst person in the world, but I didn't let that stop me. My guess is that Cassie was friends with me out of convenience and because I respected the fact that she was older and had never insulted her.

Cassie gave Janice another once-over, probably also surprised I had landed a friend who was so showy. Janice was wearing a bright blue miniskirt, a white T-shirt, and matching blue sandals. She had put her black hair up into a high ponytail like a cheerleader.

"This is my cousin, Janice," I said.

Cassie informed us that she had just hit 1,227 forehands against the backboard.

Janice laughed, her first in two days.

Cassie set her racquet bag down and balanced it between her feet. "You think I'm kidding?"

"Why would anyone even *want* to do that?" Janice asked.

"Where are you from?" Cassie asked.

"Michigan," Janice said.

"Why would you want to come here in July when it's like 150 degrees?"

"My dad wanted to get rid of me," Janice said.

The way she said it startled me. I had not asked Janice why she was at our house out of fear that it might upset her, but also because it was very clear that she wanted as little to do with me as possible. Every time we were alone, she kept the conversation to the absolute minimum, preferring to nap or read the stack of *Teen Beat* magazines she'd brought with her. She was not, in short, very companionable.

"Why?" Cassie asked Janice.

"My mom left."

"Where?" Cassie asked.

"Who knows?" Janice said. "She just took off."

Cassie looked over at me. I looked down at Janice's bright pink toenails and her blue sandals. Those are nothing special, I thought. Those are just drugstore flip-flops.

"That's terrible," Cassie said. "I mean that totally sucks."

"Tell me about it," Janice said. She put a hand up to her fringed black bangs and flipped them back out of her eyes.

"She didn't tell you where she was going?" I asked.

"Why would she tell me?" Janice replied. "She was probably afraid I'd tell him."

No one said anything. I had the urge to peel off into the woods, snake my way under the fence, and spend the rest of the afternoon alone in the fort. Maybe I would just camp out in the fort for the rest of the summer or for however long Janice was staying. No one had told me how long that would be.

"So what's there to do around here?" Janice asked Cassie.

"Not much." Cassie shrugged. "I'm in training, or I'd say we could sneak some of my mom's cigarettes and head out to the fort."

"You've never done that," I said.

"Not with you," Cassie said.

"Can you get me some?" Janice said. "I'm not in training."

"Sure thing," Janice turned to me. "Meet me in the fort in ten minutes."

Back we went under the fence. I led the way to the fort. This time Janice went right in without a peep. I laid out the tarp and she sat down. She looked me over.

"I bet you've never smoked," she said.

I shrugged.

"Well, it's easy. What you want to do is breathe in really deep, then breathe back out, and that's it. It makes you feel light-headed at first. I do it all the time. Maybe your friend will give us some extras. We can sneak off into the woods when your parents are asleep."

"My mother will catch us," I said.

"No, she won't," Janice said. "She smokes. She won't be able to smell it."

I had spent the better part of my life coughing and asking various grown-ups to roll down the window or move their cigarettes away, so it was astonishing to me that Janice even wanted to attempt it.

A couple of minutes later, Cassie returned. She had a brand-new pack of Kent's and a lighter.

"Won't your mother notice they're missing?" I said.

"She buys them by the carton," Cassie said. "Plus, she smokes a pack a day herself."

Cassie handed the pack to Janice, and Janice held it upside down and started slapping it against her other hand the way my father did.

"Do you have to do that?" I asked.

"Packs the tobacco," Cassie said.

I looked at her in wonder. All the afternoons we'd spent in the fort, and I'd never seen this side of her.

Cassie handed the pack to Janice and Janice ripped the cellophane from the top of the pack and shook one out into her hand. She lit it and inhaled deeply without coughing. She bent her neck back and blew the smoke out above us. It swirled out through the branches of the honeysuckle bush.

"You know what you're doing," I said.

"My mom smoked," Janice said. "My dad didn't use to, but he does now."

"Do you have any brothers and sisters?" Cassie asked.

Janice handed the pack back to Cassie and Cassie shook one out and lit it. She inhaled and didn't cough either.

"No," Janice said.

"That's good," Cassie said.

"Why do you say that?" Janice asked.

Cassie shrugged. "Mostly they suck."

Cassie's brother Ian was nine and a pain in the butt. One time he had emptied a whole bag of plastic spiders into her bed while she was sleeping and that wasn't even the half of it.

"I might like it actually," Janice said. "It's just going to be me and my dad now. A real laugh riot."

Cassie handed me the pack and I shook one out. I didn't really want to light it, but I felt like this was not the time to interrupt the conversation. I wanted to hear more about Janice's life.

"So, do you mind talking about it?" Cassie asked.

I lit my cigarette and took a small puff. It tasted like I had licked the asphalt, and I felt a rush of water in my mouth.

Janice shook her head. "She used to sleep all the time anyway, so when she left, it wasn't that surprising. One day I just went in after her nap to ask her a question and she was gone." She stopped and took a drag of her cigarette.

"Whoa," Cassie said after it was clear Janice wasn't going to elaborate.

"So, I called my dad," Janice finally added after taking another drag.

"And you had to wait there?" I said. "All by yourself? When did this happen?" I crushed my cigarette out in the dirt hoping no one would notice.

"I went outside and waited on the front steps." Janice took another drag, inhaling deeply. "I was nine."

"That is crazy," Cassie said.

"She *was* crazy," Janice said.

After a moment, I said, "Was she always crazy?"

"No, I don't think so," Cassie said. "She used to work for my dad, so she couldn't have been then."

"My mom was a model for a little while," I said. I didn't add, *before she was a secretary.*

"That's not work," Cassie said.

"Yes it is," I said.

"You know it's funny . . . your mom is like the opposite of my mom," Janice said. "But in a weird way, she's kind of the same."

"What do you mean?" I asked, shocked.

Just then we heard a noise. Cassie got up and stuck her head out of the opening. "Construction workers. They've got these long orange sticks, and they're coming this way." She threw her cigarette down on the ground and then stepped on it. "Let's get out of here."

I followed her out of the fort, and we ran toward the fence. I was just about to crawl through the hole when I noticed Janice wasn't behind us. Cassie had continued to the street, so I ran back toward the fort, thinking about what Janice had said about my mother. If my mother reminded Janice of her own mother, was my mother going to leave? It seemed unlikely, and yet there was something I couldn't quite pin down that troubled me. It was many years before I realized my mother's perfect veneer was just like the chocolate dip on an ice cream cone. Who knew what was happening underneath?

When I reached the fort, I knelt and stuck my head through the opening. I was about to say, "Hey, come on," when I saw Janice. She was sitting cross-legged on the tarp. She had either ashed into her hand, or the cherry of her cigarette had fallen off and she had caught it. Either way, she was sitting there staring at the burning ember in her hand as if she couldn't feel a thing.

That night at dinner my mother held her hands out for grace, and when Janice bowed her head, my mother said, "While you are staying in this house, Janice, you will say grace and hold hands."

Janice held out her hand, and when my mother saw the angry oozing welt, she got up from her chair so quickly it overturned and hit the buffet with a loud bang. Gert opened the kitchen door and asked if everything was OK.

"No, no, no!" my mother said, shaking her head briskly. "Come with me this minute, Janice."

While they were in the bathroom, I told my father and Gert what had happened.

"That poor girl," Gert made the clicking noise. "At least she won't be alone with her pain now. You are helping her through it."

"Yes, we are," my father said. "You're so right."

After Gert had gone back into the kitchen, my father picked up his fork and stabbed a piece of asparagus. "So what did you two do today?" he asked.

My mother treated Janice's wound with Bacitracin and bandaged it, and that night after we went to bed, she called Janice's father. The next day, we took Janice to the airport.

"That girl needs more help than we can give her," my mother said after Janice disappeared down the gateway to the plane. Then she smiled at me, with teeth.

AFTERWARD

When he was in the grip of it, my son would yell: "You're such a fucking bitch, Mom!"

I thought I was doing the right thing. I never responded. It was better than reacting. God knows I didn't want to tell him what I thought of him.

I kept the door locked. I closed the curtains.

Sometimes, the pounding went on for hours. "Do you know how this makes me feel?" he'd scream.

Bang.

Bang.

Bang.

And then the crying.

I ignored it all.

Did I drive him to it? What should I have done?

I knew something was wrong when I saw the voicemail. He'd never left me a voicemail before.

"Mom, you can find your son on the corner of Jefferson

and Alter in the parking lot around the back of the bank building. Mom, this is not a prank call. I'm sorry."

It sounded like a computer-generated voice. It wasn't my son's voice. Or that of any of his friends. Or even a human voice. I put the phone down and sat on my hands, which were freezing. I sat on my hands and stared out the back window at the trampoline, which had a layer of snow across the top of it. The trampoline I had bought seven years ago when he was eleven.

The day before it happened, I had requested a book from the library.

The Waves by Virginia Woolf.

The Waves was on the hold shelf, and I was on my way to pick it up when I got the call.

For days afterward, the name kept bumping up on my shore.

The waves.

The waves.

The waves.

At night I dreamed about the waves.

My tiny rowboat, useless oars dangling from the paddle clamps, and a huge wave—a seiche wave—running me down.

I am thinking about the call. How much time passed before they made the call? Could they have saved him but were too high—too . . . blasted, strung out, so undone that someone could die right beside you and . . .

I can hear him laughing. I'm sure all these words are the wrong words. Why don't I even have the right words to describe the last moments of my own son's life? How could I have been so far away at the end? On another plane, with another vocabulary, on the other side of the galaxy.

He overdosed in the house, and they carried him to the alley. That's what the police said. A couple of junkies trekking across the empty lot. They leaned him against the dumpster as if he just needed a rest. Wedged him in between the wall and the dumpster so he wouldn't fall over. The police said:

He was transported with care.

Then whoever it was—someone else's son or daughter—phoned his mother.

with care

The rowboat dream again. Except now the boat is empty. I'm not in it anymore. Just an empty rowboat and a massive wave. Where did I go? Did I jump? Have I given up? Have I already drowned? Maybe I am swimming for shore. Maybe I am swimming right into the wave.

Maybe I am just waiting to die.

I would like to kill every person in this fucking funeral home. I know they are all thinking, *this could never happen to me.*

My sister with her *how-are-you-holding-up* look.

Aunt Betsy and her simpering pink mouth and her fat arms. When she puts her puffy hands on me, I want to spit in her face.

I want to spit on her children, too. There they are, the poster children for perfect offspring.

The bachelor's in communications.

The nurse.

Aunt Betsy, your family is doing so well!

A year ago, I would have been sitting in the back row of a funeral for a heroin addict, and I would have been sure that nothing like this could ever happen to me.

"Daniel is with the Lord."

"We wish he could have stayed with us longer, but it isn't for us to understand the plan."

When I heard the Father say those words, I wanted to scream and tear my dress down the front and race up and down the aisle. If I had a bat, I would have taken his head off.

I am possessed by the Devil and I am capable of great evil.

But I don't do anything.

I just sit in my pew and shake like a leaf, Ron next to me.

We don't touch.

Not even once.

I hate him, too.

I *really* do.

The rowboat is still empty. If I am still swimming, someone should give me a medal. But why would I bother? There is a fucking seiche wave tipping the small bowl of this lake, and all the water is going to run over the side.

And a new twist last night:

Crowds on the beach.

Spectators clapping.

I can't find myself.

All I can see are the spectators standing onshore looking out at the water. I must be surfacing and going under *again and again and again.*

They are a long way off.

Why are they clapping?

I know Ron blames me. I know Ron is shuffling around the house in his bathrobe looking at the ground because he knows that if he looks up at me, he will take the coffee pot and pour the scalding liquid on my head.

He thinks that because we fought, because I was hard on Daniel, because I wouldn't let him borrow the car, because I changed the locks and called the cops on him when he robbed the Frains next door, I caused it.

I drove him to it.

I got up today, went to the bathroom, and went back to bed. Dr. Richardson stopped by just after lunch and offered me Xanax, and Ron had to hold me back because I tried to kick the man.

The wrestling injury—the very man who prescribed the Oxycontin. A murderer in my house.

And do you know what I did? Dutiful mama?

I gave him two Oxycontin every six to eight hours (or as needed), and I did it when he said he needed it . . .

. . . *and I got him more when he said he still needed it two weeks later.*

I wrote a ten-page letter to the American Medical Association, and then I wrote to the newspaper. At 4 p.m., I called his office. When the nurse said, "Doctor Richardson's office," I yelled, "Murderer!"

I spend a lot of time lying in bed thinking about my rowboat. Before I jumped or drowned or swam away, did I ever run into anyone else out on the water? If I'm not in the boat any longer, is it possible I was rescued? And why doesn't the wave ever hit the empty boat? Why the same dream every night with the wave just about to hit and then . . .

What is the meaning of this stupid dream?

We are all at the mercy of the waves.

How trite.

Even my dreams are trite.

A lifetime of drift.

That's life.

One day you the wave will engulf you as well, *fucker*.

You know what they do now? They don't bring you down to the morgue. They pull up the faces on a computer screen. They push a button and there is your beloved son, his face, the scar on his chin from that time when he was four, when he jumped off the bed and cut it open on the dresser. The little divot and the scar above his right eyebrow from the time he was eleven and fell off his bike. That was before he sold his bike. That was after the Oxycontin and before the heroin.

•

When he died he weighed 117 pounds. He was 6′2″.

Maybe if I hadn't yelled at him.

Maybe if I hadn't yelled at him to come out of his room, to pick up the dirty laundry, to turn off the computer, to make it home on time, to stop using, to stop stealing, to stop wandering off, to stop running away, to stop selling.

To stop.

That's the word I used more than any other:

Stop.

Stop.

Stop.

He was such a good boy.

Last night, the wave crashed into the rowboat. Finally. It happened in slow motion. At first the wave appeared to be pushing the boat along, then it rolled the boat. I felt like I was watching from above, from a great distance. The wave kept coming until it filled the screen of my mind and everything went blank.

I woke up.

I died.

I woke up.

I died.

I died and then

I woke up.

When he was little, we used to take naps in the afternoon. If I woke up before him, I'd roll on my side and stare into his angelic face. His skin was soft and his lips were pink and his blond hair was like a curtain over his eyes. His little hands were cupped. One time he woke up while I was watching him.

"I wish we could stay like this forever," he said.

IN THE DOGHOUSE

Leah's friend Sasha had convinced her that estate sales were a terrific way to save money. The items were cheap to begin with, and one could easily bargain them down. Leah didn't want to go because she was too broke to buy anything—even if it was on sale. In the end, she relented because she lacked an alternate plan for the day.

The sale was on Moran Road, one of the nicest streets in town. According to Sasha, ritzy addresses usually drew scads of shoppers. If they wanted to find anything worth buying, they had to arrive right at 9 a.m. They turned onto the block at 8:55. Both sides of the street were already lined with cars. A clump of dumpy-looking people were congregated on the front lawn waiting for their entry numbers. Sasha found a spot near the end of the street underneath an elm tree. All the trees on Moran were imposing, impervious to the diseases that had brought down the spindly elms on Leah's street. Pesticide, like everything else, meted out to the rich first.

The estate sale house was the only ugly one on the block,

a gray split-level with latticework running up both sides of the plywood door.

"Oh no!" Leah exclaimed when she realized which house they were headed toward.

"Whoever built this little turd of a house must have been on drugs," Sasha said as they made their way up the front walk.

For Leah, the fact that the house was unappealing wasn't the problem. It was the location. The estate sale house was right next to a beautiful redbrick colonial in which Leah's friend Tina Buhler had once lived.

Leah had been jealous of Tina Buhler. She'd met her at a Junior League meeting five years earlier when Leah's husband, Paul, was still in law school. Leah had dropped out of the Junior League when Paul decided to become a police officer instead. Although she was happy Paul was pursuing his passion, it was clear she was never going to have her own Junior League show house. Besides, she imagined some of the sustainers looked askance at his new profession. She remembered feeling a teensy bit sorry for herself when she brought the kids over to Tina Buhler's swanky house for play dates. But then she would remind herself: at least my husband isn't a drunk; at least he isn't out every night carousing with his twenty-two-year-old paralegal.

These days, Leah felt more comfortable with people of humble means like Sasha, who was married to a schoolteacher. Sasha never offered condolences when Leah said she was spending Christmas vacation at home instead of skiing in Park City.

Tina Buhler was from West Virginia. She'd met her husband, Zane, at Princeton, which she'd attended on scholarship, the first Ivy Leaguer from her town. The colonial, the Audi, and the unlimited clothing budget had been an overwhelming boon for her, but she'd always seemed ambivalent about it. She once said that even though she didn't have much when she lived there, she'd been happier in West Virginia with her family.

"People there watch out for each other," she said. "I don't get that feeling here."

Leah had commiserated with her on that front. People in Tina's snobby neighborhood always seemed bent on knocking each other down a notch. People in Leah's middle-class neighborhood, not five miles away, knew that life delivered its own blows and that friends and family were essential to cushion the fall.

In West Virginia, Tina said she had not dealt with mean neighbors like the old woman, Eunice, who lived in the ugly house next door—the same house that Leah was now approaching for the estate sale.

Leah remembered that Eunice had called the police on Tina when the children made whooping sounds in her backyard or hit a baseball over the fence or even laughed raucously for more than two minutes at a stretch.

"She hates me," Tina used to say. "She asked me where I was from, and when I said West Virginia, she said, 'Coal mining country?' in this really snide voice. She said she had a maid named Stella who looked just like me. Another time, she just came right up to me and said, 'I don't know what it's like in the hills of West Virginia, but people around here don't ride around all night on their bicycles like drunken fools and then lock themselves out of their own houses.'"

It was true that drunken bicycle riding was a recurring problem for Tina's husband, Zane. He did not hold up well at all under Eunice's scrutiny.

Now, standing in Eunice's entryway, Leah would have given anything to see Eunice's face as interlopers scurried from room to room snatching up lamps and end tables and taking down pictures. What a lame ending for that snotty old bitch, Leah thought with more than a little satisfaction.

It was only 9:05, but several people were already struggling under the weight of their acquisitions. Neon-green carpeting covered the floor in the foyer, living room, dining room, study, and staircase. The house smelled like rotting bananas, ashtrays, and smelly shoes.

"Why do old people stink?" Sasha whispered as they made their way through the foyer.

Leah shrugged. "I think it's because they lose their sense of smell. You know, it's the precursor to dementia."

"Really? Well, promise me you'll tell me when I start to reek," Sasha said before rushing up the stairs past a portly gray-haired man who had a small area rug rolled up and tucked under his arm.

Leah stood in the middle of the foyer and looked around. In the living room, two small armchairs upholstered with a pink-and-green floral print flanked the fireplace. A checked pink-and-green sofa sat opposite it. They were so bright, they seemed to be pulsing. Leah turned away and decided to head upstairs too.

In the bedroom, several women were rifling through what must have been Eunice's closet. A size 14 red taffeta dress hung from the closet door. It looked like something Nancy Reagan might have worn, albeit in a smaller size.

Leah walked around the bed and peeked out the window, which looked down directly into Tina's yard. Eunice must have sat up in this bed in the lavender terrycloth robe now being offered up for a dollar and watched Zane during one of his drunken blowouts, maybe even the final one. It was too terrible to believe. Leah closed the sheers.

Opposite the twin bed where Eunice had probably expired was an old 19-inch television on a rolling cart. No wonder she'd heard Zane outside the window. She probably couldn't get any reception on her antiquated TV. All she could hear was her inebriated neighbor stumbling around and pounding on his back door. She'd probably had all sorts of theories about Zane: the rich boy stifled by his father who resorted to alcohol and a sexy, moronic wife. In reality, Tina had been far from a moron, but how would Eunice have known that? She'd never been able to see past Tina's West Virginia twang.

Next to the bed were a Bible, a rosary, an avocado-green rotary phone, and a paperback novel called *Bones*. Someone touched Leah's shoulder. A tiny man with a pencil mustache apologized when she flinched. He just wanted to slip past to examine the phone.

"I'm a collector," he said. "I love these old rotary phones."

The basement walls were knotty pine and a full bar lined the back wall with a plaque over the top that read *Mi Casa Es Su Casa!* All sorts of mixers and tumblers and shot glasses and other party paraphernalia lined the bar. In the other corner of the room was a fireplace. The stools were the kind that spun all the way around. Leah's parents had also had a bar in their house when she was growing up and they'd had similar stools. The stools had provided Leah with a lot of entertainment when her parents were busy with their guests.

"Every time I get my hands on something, this snooty bitch slaps me down." Sasha had appeared out of nowhere carrying a blue porcelain lamp and a small red Oriental rug. "She's got the sterling and the bookshelf, but she is not getting these things."

"You have to be tough," Leah agreed.

"People are so aggressive," Sasha sighed. "Isn't this basement the best? They used to have more fun in the old days."

The patio furniture was black wrought iron with more pink-and-green floral cushions. It reminded Leah of her grandmother's house in Florida. She'd stayed with her grandmother every Christmas while her parents booked a hotel for themselves a mile away right on the beach. Her grandmother's house had looked out onto the Intracoastal Waterway. Every now and then, a manatee would make its way into the canal. A couple of times Leah had been sitting on the dock when one surfaced. They were slow and gentle-looking creatures. Of course, that's why they were nearly extinct now. If her grandmother hadn't sold the house, Leah could probably sit on the dock for weeks without spotting one. If her grandmother hadn't sold the house in the '80s, Leah would be rich. *C'est la vie.* She sat down in a wrought-iron chair and bounced a couple of times, wondering who had purchased her grandmother's patio furniture.

"I found a couple of great chairs upstairs in the bedroom,"

Sasha said when they met back up in the kitchen. "And I'm going to nab them before that witch gets her hands on them. Can you come with me to take a look?"

Leah didn't want to go back up to the bedroom, but Sasha didn't know Tina's story, and Leah didn't want to explain her reluctance, so she followed her.

The night Zane died, Eunice had told the police it was not the first time her neighbor had passed out in the yard. She told them the drinking to excess was "a nightly occurrence." She said that Zane played loud music late at night. His white trash wife didn't care what he did. She'd seen them dancing provocatively in the backyard.

According to Leah's husband, Paul, who had heard it from Bill, a fellow police officer working the night shift, Eunice had been disgusted by Zane's perpetual intoxication.

"A man with young children! Behaving like that! Night after night!"

Eunice had shrugged when she heard Zane was dead. "Not surprised," she had said.

According to Paul, the official theory was that Zane had pulled the drunken bicycle stunt on Tina one too many times. Whatever the reason, on that particular night, he had simply crawled into the tool shed instead of pounding on the back door to get into the house. The shed was way too small to contain his six-foot-three frame. When Eunice looked out the window the next morning, she saw his legs sticking out. He was wearing khakis and loafers. She recognized his feet because he always wore dark brown loafers with tassels, no socks. Tina had discovered her husband was dead when she opened the back door to take the kids to school a couple of minutes later. The police arrived before she even had a chance to call them—summoned by Eunice, of course.

Leah was happy when Tina moved back to West Virginia with her children six months later. Why should she remain in that house next to her snotty neighbor forever? Besides, she had always seemed so homesick. Since then, Leah had received only one message from her. Tina said she was happier than she'd been in a long time. She and the children were staying with her mother. All five of them had to share a two-bedroom apartment, but it was only temporary. Her estate would be settled soon, then the construction on her new house would begin.

At the checkout counter, Sasha gave Leah the keys to the car so she could pull up to the front of the house to load the chairs. As Leah walked down the block to Sasha's car, she felt bad about so many things she could barely sift through all the layers of remorse. If she hadn't been so jealous of Tina, she would have been a much better friend. She should have suggested contacting Alcoholics Anonymous or a doctor about Zane's drinking. Leah and Paul had discussed confronting Zane, but they'd never done anything. Paul, the police officer and model citizen, was always reluctant to preach or meddle in other people's business. For the most part, it was a trait Leah admired, although it certainly hadn't been the best solution in this case.

When Leah pulled up to the house, Sasha was waiting in the driveway, but she was not holding the chairs. Instead, she was glancing over her shoulder.

Leah beeped to get her attention.

"What happened to the chairs?" Leah said.

"It was crazy!" Sasha slammed the passenger door. "I can't believe what just happened."

"What?" Leah said.

"Just start driving. I hate estate sales. Why do I do this to myself?"

Leah drove down the block and turned toward the village.

"On my way to the checkout, I stopped in the den to look at some books. While I was rifling through the bookshelf, that old bitch came in the room and started yelling at me about the chairs: They were nice chairs! Why was I trying to rob her? Then the old biddy picked up the chairs and took them back up the stairs. When I told the checkout lady, she just shook her head and said she'd never held an estate sale quite like this one before. She said the owner is a total quack."

"Wait, she's still alive?"

Sasha nodded. "She doesn't have any family. Her plan is to move into assisted living after she sells everything."

"That sounds reasonable."

"Sure, but the saleslady said she showed up this morning and started giving all the salespeople a hard time—things were priced wrong, she was being robbed, she'd decided not to sell certain things—so the saleslady said to her, "Why are you having this estate sale if you don't actually want to get rid of anything?"

"She said she didn't really want to move. She was afraid her old neighbor was going to come back to town and 'take her out.' She told the saleslady that her next-door neighbor is a homicidal maniac." Sasha paused and raised her eyebrows. "But, if you ask me, that old lady is the crazy one."

"Did you ask the saleslady why she would say that?"

"Yup, the old woman told her every night her next-door neighbor's husband would get drunk, and this wife—the one she called a maniac—would send him out to the doghouse, like, literally there was a shed in the backyard. The old woman said that on the night the husband died, she saw the wife marching the husband out to the shed as usual. The old woman couldn't believe she was going to leave him out there because it was frigid outside. The next morning, she looked out the window again and there were the husband's bare feet sticking out of the shed. Frozen. She told the police the whole story, apparently, but everyone believed the wife."

SUPERMAN AT HOGBACK RIDGE

I called my wife, Teri, to tell her the car had conked out on the road to Hogback Ridge. "Serves you right!" she said. Then, she hung up on me.

It sounds harsh, but she had a point. I should have given up on this clunker long ago. My Volvo 240 is nearly fifteen years old, and I had been trying to hold on until I hit the three-hundred-mile mark. I'd replaced the fuel pump the week before, but clearly, that wasn't the problem. Suddenly, on Route 307, the car was refusing to go faster than ten miles per hour. Not good to coast to a stop on a rural road out by Hogback Ridge State Park, but better than zeroing out in the middle of the highway, I figured.

Teri had just bought a new car for herself, and I admit I was holding it against her, refusing to replace mine because she'd acted so imprudently. The Lexus was way beyond our means, especially if we planned to retire in seven years as we had discussed ad infinitum.

My son, David, fifteen, was beside me in the passenger seat. Ear buds in 24/7. Let's just say, he was there, but not there. This fishing trip was a means of luring him back, no pun intended. When he was younger, Hogback Ridge had always been one of our favorite destinations, 414 acres bordered on the north by the Grand River and the south by Mill Creek. The Grand is home to more than seventy species of fish. Plus, the river is bounded on one side by a high narrow ridge, which in the winter clearly resembles the bony spine of a hog, and in the early spring, when the steelhead are running, is overlaid with delicate white bloodroot and spring beauty flowers.

I decided to try to coast downhill into the parking lot. Because of the slight decline, we were cruising at a cool 10 mph when I looked in the rearview mirror and saw a black pickup truck barreling down the road at 80–90 mph. I turned my wheel toward the side of the road and the entrance to the long-abandoned Thunder Bay Golf Course, though there was no way I could make it out of his way in time. My only hope was that he would see me and slam on the brakes, which he did. He came to a stop about two feet before impact. Before I could even release my grip on the wheel, he screeched out into the other lane and pulled up alongside me.

I rolled down the window.

"Fuck you, grandpa, what the fuck? What the fuck are you doing *sitting* in the fucking road?" The driver was a teenager with light blue, red-rimmed eyes, a shaved head, a nose ring, and earrings that ran like ladder rungs up and down his earlobes. He scowled at me, and I noticed his right front incisor was missing and the rest of his teeth were dung brown.

The person in the passenger seat leaned forward, a pasty young girl with a nose ring whose hair was concealed by a white ski hat with a pink pom-pom. "You fucking loser," she yelled. "Why don't you learn to drive? Get the fuck out of the road."

I glanced over at David. He was staring at them, but his ear buds were still in. I hoped he couldn't hear them through his music. I turned away without responding. It's not wise to interact with insane people. I have a button under my desk at the bank that I have used twice to diffuse situations much like this one. My son might be recalcitrant, but at least he's not a skinhead, I thought. If parents don't occasionally pad the pros and ignore the cons, this job can seem pretty thankless.

At least, David wasn't as openly hostile to me as he was to Teri. She's a high school principal, so you might assume that no surly teen could flummox her, but nothing could be further from the truth. The strain of David was nearly killing her. In fact, I think it was worse for her because kids at her school were always confiding in her, telling her she was so much more understanding than their parents. Since David was now effectively mute, the three of us spent most of our evenings sealed off in separate rooms—me in my upstairs office, Teri in the TV room competing in the Netflix Olympics, and David down in the basement gaming.

After the skinhead had doused me with vitriol one last time, he rolled up his window and peeled out ahead of us. Thank God that's over, I thought, and I started to loosen my grip on the wheel. But then a few yards down the road, he must have decided that he had more to say, because he stopped again, got out of his car, and started marching down the middle of the road toward me. The girl remained in the car. I noticed the license plate read *GoFast1*. The skinhead was at least six feet tall. Skinny. Pale as shaved ice. Combat boots. Tattoos covering every inch of skin right up to his neck.

"What about it, old man?" he called out as he approached.

Did he think I wanted to fight? While he stared down at me with his rheumy blue eyes, his arms jerked up and down like a marionette who was being yanked around by a sadistic puppeteer.

There was no escaping the guy. My car had slowed to 5 mph, if that. We were on a flat stretch. The doors were locked, but I doubted they would save us. David took out one of his ear buds and asked, "What's going on?"

"This guy's a real jerk," I said.

Then, just as he was about to lean into my window and do who knows what, I heard three beeps. Teri had pulled up behind us in her shiny black Lexus. I had never doubted she would come to rescue us. Though we were annoyed at each other, we had not slipped down the next notch to complete indifference or contempt. Not yet, at least. I had seen that transformation many times in couples we've known and when I've counseled people separating their assets. Teri and I used to thank our lucky stars we had not succumbed to that.

The skinhead looked over at Teri.

"Shut the fuck up, you rich bitch," he said. Then he glared down at me one last time, flipped me off again, and turned back toward his truck.

"That was weird," David said. He put his ear buds back in.

My cell phone rang. "Who was that guy?" Teri asked.

Since David wasn't listening, I explained what had happened as we slowly crawled toward the parking lot, Teri bringing up the rear.

"That's crazy! What did David say?"

"He's not even on location." I glanced over at him. As usual he was staring blankly at his screen.

"Well, for once, I'm glad to hear it."

David's video game addiction had ramped up over the past six months, taking over his whole life. We had time limits, but he kept circumventing them. Do your homework first, we said. No gaming except on the weekends, we said. But if we weren't home—if Teri had a late meeting or we were out to dinner—what was he doing? You guessed it. Where were his friends? We didn't know.

He said his friends were "in the game."

"One day you're going to wake up and you'll have spent an entire decade in the basement," Teri said.

Of course, that didn't faze him at all.

Sometimes, I tried to inspire him. I told him stories of our Irish ancestors, how they'd come over in the 1860s in a boat. How they'd survived the potato famine. My father was the son of a Cleveland firefighter. He had worked his way up from stock boy to salesclerk. Eventually he bought his own hardware store. What I was trying to convey was that people needed survival skills. There had to be a point to one's existence, even if that point, in my case, was simply working in a bank, bringing home a paycheck.

"Did you dream about becoming a banker when you were a little kid?" he'd asked me one time. The disdain in his voice made me clench my fists.

"No one dreams about becoming a banker," I said. "I was lucky to have options though. I can tell you that."

What I didn't tell him was that I had wanted to be an artist, the least practical profession in the world. The reason I didn't pursue it was because one professor, Mr. Holman, had looked over a couple of my pen and ink drawings and said, "Well, I wouldn't exactly call you precocious." I switched into the business school the next day.

We finally ended up taking David's computer. We left it at his grandmother's house. In response, he refused to study at all. His grades plummeted. He spent whole weekends in bed. After that, we tried therapy. Part of his behavior was pure teenager, according to the psychologist. Part of it was still under investigation. David was currently undergoing testing. The only thing he had revealed to the therapist was that sometimes he got scared "for no reason."

Since David's metamorphosis, Teri had been depressed. Out of the blue, she bought the Lexus. "I'm fifty years old," she said, "and I've never had a decent car." I shouldn't have made her feel bad about it, but inside I was seething. How were we going to retire early if she made such expensive impulse purchases?

My car came to a full stop as soon as we reached the parking lot; it was all I could do to maneuver it into a space. It turned out the space was right next to the lowlife's pickup truck. The driver and the girl with the pom-pom hat had just emerged from it. When I parked, the skinhead was pulling on his waders.

"Did you have to park right next to them?" David asked.

"I didn't have much of a choice. We'll just wait until they leave."

In order to avoid making eye contact, I reached over David and opened the glove box pretending to look for something. After a few minutes, out of the corner of my eye, I saw the skinhead stomp off toward the porta potty. A quick glance around the parking lot revealed two other cars, as well as a ranger's truck and Teri's Lexus.

"I'm going to talk to your mother," I said to David.

"Are you serious? You're getting out of the car?" When he looked at me, I saw that his face was devoid of disgust for once, and without that overlay, he looked like the old David.

"He went to the bathroom. There are other people here. Nothing will happen with all these witnesses. Lock the doors after I get out."

I slammed the door and started walking toward Teri's car. I heard David lock the doors behind me.

Either the skinhead had the world's smallest bladder, or he'd decided against using the facilities. He emerged from the porta potty before I'd gone ten steps.

"Well, hello, sir, you piece of crap, asshole, how the fuck are you?" he asked as he approached me.

I continued with my strategy of non-engagement. I was wondering why Teri had chosen to park so far away from me, but then I noticed that she had pulled in right next to a Yukon with a park ranger's logo on it. As I continued my death march toward her, I saw that she was talking to the ranger. The skin-head must have noticed the ranger, too, because he suddenly stopped in his tracks. "Nice driving, douchebag," he muttered to me before turning back toward his own truck.

Teri and the ranger were standing in between their two cars. Teri's not a small woman, but the ranger was at least six inches taller, his face blocked out by a bushy red beard. His belly was so big it looked as if there might be another person lodged inside him. As I approached, he nodded to me and asked if I was OK.

"Sure," I said. "I'm OK."

"Are you *sure?*" His red eyebrows rose.

"That was not OK." Teri shook her head. Her blonde hair was matted to her forehead as if she'd just returned from a long run. "That kid is insane. Did you hear him just now?"

The ranger looked calmly in the direction of the skinhead. "Why don't I go check it out," he said.

"I'd like to kill that kid," Teri said, her narrowed eyes drilling into the skinhead. Teri's anger, which appears quite regularly these days, is a new feature. I'm not sure exactly when it happened, but I have my theories. When we married twenty years ago, we had similar long-term goals. I was going to work until I was fifty-nine and retire on what I projected by then would be a hefty 401K. Teri was going to retire at the same time after thirty years in education with a sizable pension. We were in lockstep, but then one of her coworkers, a science teacher and marathoner, dropped dead the day after his fifty-fourth birthday three years ago. Soon after, Teri insisted we take a vacation. A real one. Not in a tent. She wanted to see Europe, she wanted to cruise, she wanted to live a little. We argued. Then about a year later, Teri's assistant principal, Mary Ellen, leaned down to retrieve a cup that had fallen over in her car and ran right into the back of a semitruck. Teri signed up for a transcendental meditation class. She started doing yoga. And then the clincher, this past fall: a boy named Thomas, whom Teri had been very close to and whom she had been trying to help navigate a serious bout of depression, went home for lunch after an algebra test and shot himself in the head. Teri had to make the difficult decision to announce the suicide over the PA during sixth hour before social media revved up. This meant that students who had been sitting next to Thomas in his morning classes were traumatized, and their parents were outraged because they had not been notified first. Teri had to go before the school board and defend her decision. She had weathered it, but since then she had become more and more agitated at home. A sock on the ground. A spoon in the sink. Anything might set her off. I was trying to simply live through her mood swings when one day she announced we should start seeing a therapist to discuss our divergent worldviews. And now the "we" has morphed into "me." It feels to "me" as if Teri and the therapist have ganged up on me. *What do you want? What do you want? What do you want?* they always ask, as if I haven't told Teri a million times. When I remind them that I want to retire, Teri always shakes her head. "I mean now," she says. "I'm talking about right *now*."

The skinhead was standing next to the driver's side door putting on a fishing vest as the ranger approached him.

"Well, hello, officer," he said. "How are you doing today?"

"I hear you have been giving this man a hard time?" The officer pointed over his shoulder.

The skinhead smiled wearily at me as if I were just a guy sitting on the other side of the table during a loan negotiation. "This man was stopped in the middle of the road. I admit I lost my temper, but I was never disrespectful."

Before I even had a chance to respond, Teri shouted. "He's lying!"

Two fishermen, young guys, were standing next to a white Dodge minivan watching the scene unfold. If worse came to worst—the park ranger, me, these two guys—I figured we could take the skinhead out.

"You were going eighty miles an hour," Teri shouted. "And you were NOT respectful."

"Officer, at no time did I act disrespectfully. I was not going eighty miles an hour. If I was, I would have hit that man because *he* was parked in the middle of the road." The skinhead smiled at me again and put a hand over his heart as if he were planning to recite the Pledge of Allegiance.

"Yeah," said the girl with the pink pom-pom. "Garth was as nice as could be." She turned and glared at Teri, who glared right back.

"You did not act respectfully," Teri repeated. "You called him all sorts of names. You were driving at a terrific speed. You were mocking him, and at one point you got out of the car and harassed him."

The park ranger looked at Teri. "Would you like me to call the police? We can call the police."

The pom-pom girl cocked her head at Teri. "I'm sorry, is there a reason you're involved? Can we help you in some way?"

"Yes," Teri said. "That is my husband, and you need to apologize."

The girl took two steps toward Teri. Teri took two steps toward her.

"I'll handle this." The park ranger held his hand up to stop them.

He turned to Teri. "Ma'am, can you just give me a minute here?"

"This is insane." Teri turned to me. "Where's David?"

We both glanced over at my car. David was still sitting in the passenger's seat of my car, ear buds imbedded. On Mars.

One time during the "inspirational speech" phase of my dealings with David, I told him about my great-grandfather who had fought in World War I. My great-grandfather was a first-generation Irish immigrant who lived on Kimberley Avenue in Cleveland in a duplex with his parents and six siblings. Next door was a family of Russian immigrants named Siegel, who had a batch of kids as well, one of whom grew up to be Jerry Siegel, the creator of Superman. Jerry was just a young boy during World War I, but in one interview years later, he mentioned that he had been in awe of the soldiers who lived on his street during the Great War. From that statement, I had embellished the story a bit for David's sake.

"Do you realize that your great-grandfather was one of the soldiers who sparked the creation of Superman? His bravery, his integrity, his comportment was the catalyst for the young creator. You need to think about the impact you want to have on the world. You need to think about how you will make your contribution."

When David asked me whether I'd always wanted to be a banker, I should have told him the truth. I wanted to be Superman. I grew up hearing my grandfather's story, and I always thought I'd get my chance to do something extraordinary. Later, I considered myself lucky that I'd never been tested.

"I have to call a tow truck. Why don't you wait in your car and I'll call you when I get through?" I said to Teri.

"Good idea." She marched back toward her car. I got back into mine, locked the door, and dialed AAA. Immediately, I was put on hold.

After a few minutes, the park ranger knocked on my window. Beyond him, the skinhead and the pom-pom girl had gathered up their poles and were heading for the trail that leads down to the river.

"The car is registered to the driver," the ranger said. "He's eighteen years old with no priors. They said they won't bother you. I'll tell you what, road rage is really on the rise around here." He shook his head.

"This wasn't ordinary road rage," I said. "I think they're on something."

The ranger nodded his head in agreement. "That might be. Do you want me to call the cops?"

"If he has nothing on his record, what will they do?"

"Not much."

"Seems kind of pointless then."

He shrugged.

"No need to call the cops," I said.

"I'll go tell your wife things are under control," he said.

I rolled the window back up.

David took out his ear buds. "Meth," he said.

"Meth? You think they're on meth?"

He nodded. "His license plate is GoFast1, and 'go fast' is a nickname for meth. He's from Ohio, which is like meth central, he looks like he hasn't eaten in years, and he's mean." He said all of this without looking at me. "Mom shouldn't have messed with him."

I looked out the window. The park ranger pulled out of his spot and waved as he passed by on his way out of the parking lot. The menaces had reached the trail at the edge of the parking lot. I glanced over at Teri's car. There was no one left in the parking lot except for our two cars and the skinhead's pickup.

"Hello, may I help you?"

I had forgotten I was on hold with AAA.

"Yes," I said. "I need a tow truck . . ."

Before I could finish the sentence, I heard someone yell.

David took out one of his ear buds.

"That's Mom," he said, though how he had heard her through the cacophony of sound coming from his ear buds, I have no idea.

"Are you sure?" I opened my car door.

Teri was standing next to her car. "Hey you!" she was yelling to the receding back of the skinhead. "Hey, you!"

The skinhead stopped walking. I looked over at David in disbelief. But David was no longer in the seat next to me. His door was open. As I turned back toward my window, I saw him fly past.

"MOM!" he yelled. "Stop!"

It was the first time I'd heard David say the word *mom* in

so long that it took me a moment to remember *mom* was a word in his lexicon.

The skinhead was facing Teri now, standing about ten yards away from her. He put a hand up to his backpack strap and shimmied it off his shoulder. He unzipped the backpack and reached inside.

"Mom!" David yelled again. "Come here right now! We have to go. I'm late. Remember? We have to leave right NOW."

Teri looked back at David. I'm sure the word *mom* had stunned her as well. When David reached her, he took hold of her arm and propelled her back toward her car.

I got out of my car and hurried over to Teri's car, keeping an eye on the skinhead. He was still standing with his hand in the backpack watching Teri and David as they ran away from him, looking bemused at their extreme agitation. Then he saw me crossing the parking lot. And he pulled out the gun.

"Can I help you, you dumb fuck? If you want something, I got just the thing." He waved the gun back and forth, and I have to admit, I wasn't sure I could make it to the car. I'm ashamed to say I lost control of my bladder.

Teri was just opening the driver's side door and David was heading toward the back door, their backs toward the gun. I kept walking quickly toward them, not knowing if or when he planned to shoot and wondering if the wetness had reached the outside of my pants. But he didn't do anything. He seemed to simply enjoy the fact that he had scared the daylights out of me.

"Mom, you should *never* have taken a chance like that. Never. Never. *Never*," David was saying as I slid into the passenger seat. "That guy could have had a gun."

There was a large manila envelope sitting on the seat, and I put it in my lap to cover my pants keeping my eyes on the skinhead. At the same time, Teri finished buckling her seat belt and looked over at me. When I didn't turn my head to acknowledge her, she must have followed my gaze out through the windshield to the skinhead who was still pointing the gun right at us.

"Holy shit," she said.

"Mom, start the car!" David leaned up next to Teri. "Mom, you have to turn the key."

But Teri didn't move, and I'm sorry to say, I didn't either.

David leaned over from the back seat and turned the key in the ignition. "I know you're scared, Mom, but you've got to drive," he said. "*Now.*"

Teri put her foot on the gas, and we peeled out of the parking lot. I was still unable to move my head, but I could see out of my peripheral vision that her hands were clamped to the wheel as if they'd been soldered on.

There was a moment when we were racing away from the skinhead but were still in range that I realized David's head was a perfect target if the skinhead chose to take a shot.

"David," I said. "Get down."

My words did not come out with any conviction. I am not sure David even heard me. My voice was just the trickle of a voice, soft and insubstantial. Not up to the task at all. I remembered that my father, the war hero, had once said, "You never know how you'll react in a life-and-death situation until you're in one."

Now I knew.

I also knew how David would respond. Even if I hadn't been capable of it, my son had risen to the occasion. It almost canceled out my own feelings of inadequacy.

Almost.

WHY DID I EVER THINK THIS WAS A GOOD IDEA?

Bridget Flanagan stood in the middle of what used to be her studio. A discordant sound (could it really be called music?) was coming from her son William's room directly above her head. She could ask him to turn it down, but that would require interacting with him, possibly screaming at the top of her lungs. She couldn't bear the thought, so she remained amid the thumping and screeching surrounded by shopping bags.

The extra bedroom had not been used as an actual studio since Bridget had worked as a graphic artist for J. Walter Thompson. They'd allowed her to work from home briefly after her oldest child, Keira, was born. Those were the days when it had been impossible to stand at the easel or sit at her desk for more than three minutes at a stretch without Keira letting out a rebel yell. Then, two years later, along came Brendan. William, the surprise, arrived a week after Brendan started kindergarten. In the baby years, it had not even been a question—her children cried, and she responded. In those days, her main goal was to do everything differently than her own mother. She didn't want her own children to know what it felt like to be someone's last priority. Now, the joke was on her. More often than not, she was the one crying, and they could not have cared less.

The extra bedroom had functioned as a storage unit since she'd given notice to J. Walter almost two decades before. Briefly, when the kids first went to school, Bridget had thought about turning it back into an art studio, but somehow, with the lunchtime volunteering and the various sports commitments and the intermittent childhood dramas, that had never happened. Even so, it had not been a dump (her husband Ryan's term) until last year, when Bridget began shopping while on college tours with William.

It had seemed like every single town sported an outlet mall, and that had been her solace when William, ear buds permanently embedded, ignored her many attempts at conversation.

Everything she had purchased over the past twelve months was piled high in the room. On top of that, William had decided he wasn't going to college right away; he was going to take a "leap year" or a "gap year" or whatever kids called loafing around doing nothing.

"His meal ticket is running out," Ryan said. "Someone ought to clue him in."

It turned out that not only did William have an alternate plan, but he'd actually saved enough from his computer repair business to buy a roundtrip ticket to Beijing. Scrapping college was nothing Bridget's other two children had even contemplated. They had gone, no questions asked. Keira had ended up at Colby, and as soon as she'd graduated, she'd moved to New York City. Now she lived a life of self-imposed poverty in Brooklyn, working temp jobs and trying to start her own web design business. Brendan had attended Georgetown, and then landed as a legislative aide on the Hill. Since Brendan was five years older than William, the other two had been gone for what seemed like a lifetime. For his entire high school career, William had had his parents to himself.

Well, good riddance, she thought when William told her he planned to see the Great Wall. It was a terrible thing to think, and she knew it, but if anyone spent more than five minutes with William, they wouldn't judge her. No, that was not true, either. The truth was that William was kind—a better word might be obsequious—to everyone except her. He saved all of his vitriol for Bridget, the softie who had purchased the entire Harry Potter LEGO series and the expensive trampoline, which he wasted no time riddling with BB pellets. A few years later, she'd been the sucker to outfit "his" rec room with a leather sectional, only to walk in on him several days later slitting the underside open with a pocketknife to hide pot.

There was nothing to be done about it now. In a week he would be gone. The ticket was open-ended, and though he had not decided when he was coming back, in theory he was supposed to start college the following August at Oberlin.

Now, Bridget turned her attention to the shopping bags. It was astonishing to see exactly how much she had acquired.

She hadn't opened any of them. Every time she bought something new, she simply dumped it in the studio.

The initial shopping spree had been at an art supply store, where she'd filled several bags with tubes of oil paints, colored pencils, charcoal pencils, various brushes, and linen for canvases. Then she'd hit a bookstore, where she'd headed straight for *The Art of Abstract Painting*, *The New Artist's Manual*, and *The Painterly Approach*, veering off to the self-help section for *My Nest Isn't Empty: It Just Has More Closet Space* and *Chicken Soup for the Soul: Empty Nesters*, then on to *Barefoot Contessa* and *The Guide to Eating Mindfully*. Somewhere along the line, she'd succumbed to the lure of the clothing stores as well.

The first thing that caught her eye as she entered the room were all the art books she'd bought spilling out onto the floor. William, who had been listening to a headache-inducing rap station in his bedroom, must have fallen asleep, because now there was '70s music blaring above Bridget's head. Maybe he had fallen into a submarine sandwich–induced coma. Every morning, he woke up early, mowed his lawns, came home with two submarine sandwiches, and pounded up to his room to sleep the rest of the day before heading out with friends just about the time Bridget was going to bed.

Whatever the reason for the new station, Bridget was grateful for five minutes of relative quiet. She stood and faced the bags lining the back wall, which were stacked horizontally from the floor to just above the windowsill. She would have to be careful when she removed the first one or the whole heap might cascade down. As she latched onto a tiny bag at the top, she realized that "Dancing Queen" by ABBA had come on the station. It used to be her favorite song in high school. She grabbed the handle and shuffle danced around in a circle. For a small bag, it was surprisingly heavy. She put it down and cleared a space in the middle of the room.

"Dancing queen, young and sweet, only seventeen, yea you can dance, you can sing, having the time of your life."

Bridget closed her eyes and twirled around in the tiny space available to her amid the rubble. Wouldn't it be great to spin back to seventeen, to flip-flops and short shorts?

The last time she heard "Dancing Queen," she'd been on an exchange program in London. She had worked for TV-am on the weekends and once sat opposite Prince Andrew during an interview. When she got home, she told everyone he'd been flirting with her. She'd said it so often it felt true. She had even sketched him and still had the drawing. ABBA had been playing on the ferry from Dover to Amsterdam when Bridget was taking a weekend trip with a boy, who, when she was high, bore a marked resemblance to Tom Cruise. They'd never had anything to say to each other. She couldn't even remember his name, but she could still envision his abs, which were miraculous.

Decades had passed since then. When she and Ryan were first married and she'd moved to his hometown, fresh from her travel adventures, her mother-in-law, Toni, would share anecdotes about her own junior year in Paris. How pathetic, Bridget had thought. She's talking about that trip like it was yesterday.

She should ask Ryan to go dancing sometime. It wasn't that much to ask. There were plenty of things she did for him that didn't appeal to her—golf, gin rummy, driving to Frankenmuth for chicken dinners came to mind. As she danced, she opened her eyes briefly to make sure she wasn't going to collide with anything and saw that someone was standing in the doorway.

She stopped mid-spin and nearly toppled over. It was William. How long had he been there? He was staring at her, scowling from beneath his long greasy bangs. The room wobbled.

"You looked sooooo stupid, Mom," he said, shaking his head before turning and walking away.

Bridget, deflated, abandoned the studio, closing the door on the mess. She went upstairs to her room and slipped under the covers. There she lay with her palms up, staring at the ceiling light.

Bridget had grown up in a large city on the East Coast surrounded by her parents and their friends and all of their monstrous ambitions. At cocktail parties, imposing men with cigars talked about this deal and that. The women discussed travel and art shows, the books they were writing, the weight they were losing, the jewelry they were making, the PR firm they had just opened, the charity they had devoted their lives to promoting. Bridget stood amid the clatter of silver trays and the swoosh of their ominously puffy fur coats and the nauseating plumes of smoke. It seemed to her that they were like great colorful bubbles floating through the room, completely encapsulated, each unable to see beyond their own illuminated orb.

Bridget's mother was one of the most splendiferous bubbles. She painted, she wrote, she chaired organizations. All of her telephone conversations began like this:

"Well, I'm onto something new . . . it's going to be terrific if we can get it off the ground."

"I've been working like a dog . . ."

"I really think this is going to be sensational . . ."

"I'd love to get together, but I'm just swamped with the new account . . ."

"How about we go to the zoo a week from Thursday, Bridget? Let's put that in our calendars, and then, unless the Frye deal goes through, it's definitely a date."

Bridget had decided early on that she would never make her children feel like they were curios hung on the wall next to the coats at parties. Unlike her mother, she would devote her life to her family. For a while it had seemed like a great plan. She'd been proud of herself for breaking the chain, but now she wasn't sure whether she'd achieved all that much. She'd behaved with great restraint, it was true. But it was possible that by trying to avoid her mother's mistakes, she'd gone too far in the other direction. If she'd said something snide to her mother, her mother would have shot a poison dart right back at her. One time she'd told her mother to leave her alone, and her mother had slapped her so hard that the hand imprint lasted eight hours. Her mother had won a momentary victory by silencing her outbursts, but she had paid the ultimate price: a daughter who avoided her at all costs.

Bridget was proud of the fact that her first two children actually missed her when she left the house. They told her what they had been up to at school. Keira liked a boy named Rod the entire time she was in grade school. Eight years of Rod, Rod, Rod. Brendan had wanted to start his own fly-fishing business since they lived in an area where fly-fishing was the rage and she'd made sure he had all the supplies, helped him advertise. When he graduated, salutatorian, he'd said she was the most important influence in his life.

But it had all been so short-lived. Both Brendan and Keira had left home without a glance back, and even though William had been sweet when he was younger, for the last two years he'd made her miserable with his late nights and ranting temper tantrums. After all the sacrifices, what did Bridget have now? She had twenty extra pounds, blank canvases, and a husband who spent all of his waking life on the golf course. It was not that she'd expected something in return, per se, but she had expected to forge deep connections, something to fill the void. She'd wanted her children to know they mattered, but perhaps she had needed to feel that as well.

A few minutes later, Bridget was awakened by what sounded like quacking. Where in the world was it coming from? She shot up in bed and looked around. It was her iPhone.

"Hello?" she asked.

On the other end, William was laughing. "It's called the 'duck' ringtone, Mom. I changed it while you were sleeping. Isn't it hilarious? Can you come downstairs? I have a quick question for you."

Bridget dragged herself out of bed. Why was she even going downstairs? Maybe he really was a narcissist; what other explanation could there be for a boy who would run his mother through a shredder one minute and then call her the next minute as if nothing had happened at all?

Down in the kitchen, William asked, "Can you believe I leave in six days?"

"Nope," Bridget said, aghast at the mountain of dirty dishes in the sink. Where had they all come from?

"You know I was thinking . . . I was going through my stuff. Do you think we could go shopping one of these days?"

When he put a hand on her shoulder, Bridget tried not to flinch. "So just a minute ago I was 'soooo stupid,' and now you want to go shopping?" she asked.

"I know, Mom. I felt terrible about that. I don't know why I said it. You're the best." He removed his hand and went over to the cupboard to extract yet another bowl.

"Do you have any idea how mean you are sometimes?"

"It was just funny to see you dancing."

Funny.

Bridget woke up the next morning to what sounded like a gorilla slashing through the jungle. It took her a minute to realize it was just her own son running down the hall. His feet going down the stairs sounded like boulders tumbling off a cliff during an avalanche. Why couldn't he be thoughtful? Didn't he know that there were other people on the planet and that they might need sleep?

Now that he had made it downstairs before her, there would be no chance to make coffee before facing him. From the kitchen below, she heard a plate clatter on the granite countertop, the dishwasher open and slam shut repeatedly, a pot clanking on the stove, and the television switched on, the volume increasing to a deafening range.

Bridget opened another cupboard and noticed he had used every last cup. "I mean what is this mess? When I went to bed last night, the kitchen was clean."

"Some of the guys came over to watch a movie," he said. "Sorry about that. I'll take care of it after I do my lawns."

"When will that be exactly?" Bridget asked.

"I'll be back around 11."

Bridget had taken Tylenol PM. Perhaps that was why she felt so fuzzy. "I hope you didn't wake your father," she said.

"He didn't come down," William said with a shrug. "Anyway, I really need some new shoes. It could be fun to go shopping later today. We could go out to the mall, and then we could stop into Jeepers."

Bridget raised her eyebrows.

"Kidding!" William said, with a grin.

For years William had been obsessed with Jeepers, the indoor amusement park at the mall. Bridget would take him along with a friend at least once a month. How she had hated Jeepers! The loud whizbanging of the machines, the incessant chiming and bells that signaled success at the pinball machine, the inevitable shrieking when someone dropped their popcorn or their candy or when the small roller coaster provoked nausea.

During those outings, Bridget would sit in a booth with a book while William and his friend ran through the maze of gadgets, returning sporadically to collect more Jeepers coins.

"Brother, the things I've done for you," Bridget said.

"I know it, Mommy. I love you." William bent down to kiss the top of her head.

This is all for the shoes, she thought, and I'm licking it up like rotten milk.

At Jeepers later that afternoon, Bridget asked the attendant at the front door if they could just walk through once for old times' sake. Immediately the noise hit her like a slap. The zooming, screaming kids, the slushy machine whirring. She wanted to stick her fingers in her ears and scream.

She and William walked over to the miniature roller coaster. One boy, around four or five, was riding in a car, looping around and around. He rode with his arms in the air, and every time he passed his harried-looking mother, he yelled, "Whoa!"

"Whoa! Look at you!" she called. Then, when he was out of sight, she glanced down at her phone for a second. But a second was all she got, because around he came again.

"Whoa!" they both called out to each other.

William looked over at Bridget, and they both laughed. "This roller coaster used to seem enormous!" he said. The pint-sized car came to a halt and the little kid jumped off. William looked like a giant standing next to him.

"You never stopped screaming," Bridget said. "You screamed from the moment they put you on until I pulled you off."

"In fear?"

Bridget shook her head. "All of these kids would be crying and having meltdowns on the little tilt-a-whirl or this tiny ride here and you'd be running from one end to the other like 'What's next?!' No fear at all."

"I wish I felt that way now," William said, still looking at the kid and his mother. The kid was trying to convince his mother to stay for one more ride. The mother kept saying it was time to go, but the kid wasn't having it.

Something in his tone made Bridget pause. Was he scared now? That thought hadn't occurred to her. Her anger toward him lately had been so all-encompassing, her energy had been used up just surviving this stage. She hadn't spent time analyzing what was behind all the nastiness.

Before she could give it more thought, William clapped her on the back. "I'm ready to hit Red Robin."

In Red Robin, William ordered not one but two cheeseburgers, the sweet potato fries, and a large chocolate milkshake. He told her that in China he would stay in hostels that cost ten dollars a night.

"That sounds impossible," Bridget said.

"I know. Too good to be true, right?" he shoved a fry into his mouth and looked around. In the corner, a teenage girl with a frizzy ponytail was being serenaded by the waiters for her birthday.

"Won't you get lonely?" Bridget asked.

"Hostels are great places to meet people. Plus, I'll have Zack with me for the first leg of the trip."

"But why China? I just don't get it." It was sad that he was leaving this week and she'd never asked this question before, but then again, it's hard to know anything about a person who refuses to speak with you.

"I want to see the Great Wall. One time in AP World

History, Mr. Anderson read a poem by Mao Zedong: 'He who doesn't reach the Great Wall is no hero.' For some reason, that line really hit me. If I can make it to the Great Wall, I can do anything."

Later that night, Ryan said, "Your problem is that you let him walk all over you. One minute you're crying because he's making fun of you, and the next minute, you're out buying him new clothes."

This was true, Bridget knew, but what was there to say in response? Her behavior was inexplicable.

That night in bed, Bridget tried to envision William as a baby napping in this very bed. She remembered how, in those days, she used to pray that he would fall asleep for at least ten minutes so she could rest. On the rare occasions when he did, she'd turn toward him and study his beautiful face. Sometimes she'd pick up his tiny fingers one by one and gaze at them.

When she opened her eyes, Ryan was staring down at her as he tied his tie, his shirt bulging over his ample stomach. "What are you up to today?" he asked.

"That depends. I was going to clean out the guest room, but William put a damper on my cleaning project, so now I'm lacking motivation."

"You're supposed to take it in stride, remember?"

Bridget tried not to roll her eyes. Ryan's version of "taking it in stride" was drinking beer and watching *Curb Your Enthusiasm*.

"Maybe it just eats at me the way he's morphed into the antichrist."

"That's nothing new," Ryan said, sitting down to put on his shoes. He went into the closet. "I told you how mean I was to my mother. He'll grow out of it," he said.

How comforting, Bridget thought.

Finally, the day of departure arrived. The night before, William and his friends had partied in the basement until nearly 3 a.m. Although she and Ryan both had earplugs in, they could feel the vibrations from the TV, which was blaring noise from some apocalyptic video game.

"The only reason I'm not going down there is this is the last night we will have to deal with this," Ryan had whispered around 2 a.m.

Bridget had resolved not to wake William up the following morning. If he missed his flight, it was his problem. But the next morning she came down to see his duffel packed and waiting next to the front door. There were no dishes in the sink or in the basement. Apparently, William didn't actually want to burn the house down on his way out.

William, himself, was up and showered with a half hour to spare before his 10 a.m. departure for the airport. He had remembered his Chinese/English dictionary and his passport. The car on the way to the airport was filled with several rounds of false cheer and good wishes. Ryan handed William a small envelope, which contained the locations and phone numbers of all the American consuls in China.

At the security gate, they met up with William's friend Zack, who was accompanying him on the first two months of the journey, as well as Zack's parents, who had come to see him off.

William hugged Bridget, then Ryan. "I'm going to miss you guys," he said.

"You too," Ryan and Bridget both said.

And then, how was it possible? Suddenly it was true. Bridget could barely hold back her tears. She could not have been more surprised.

Zack hugged his parents and the boys got into the security line.

"There they go," Zack's mother said. She looked at Bridget and shrugged. Then she looked at her watch.

"We've got to run," she said. Their youngest son had a playoff baseball game at noon. With four children still at home, they might not even notice Zack was missing. Bridget remembered that she'd been so busy, she'd registered just the tiniest blip of sadness when Keira left home.

Zack's parents departed, but Ryan and Bridget stood and waited as Zack and William wound round and round through the security line. William had his small duffel slung over his shoulder. It was going to be hot in Beijing, so he'd only packed shorts and T-shirts. Maddeningly, in the end, he'd decided not to take the new sneakers they'd purchased at the mall because he didn't want to ruin them.

Finally, they made it to the security guard and handed over their passports. Bridget watched William take off his shoes. She hoped he wouldn't forget to pick his passport back up after it went through the scanner. She stood up on her tiptoes to try to get a better look. She would be surprised if she didn't get a frantic call from Asia at some point because he'd lost some vital document. Just a month ago he'd misplaced his keys to the pickup, and Ryan had had to pay $600 to replace the locks.

Once they'd picked up their bags and replaced their shoes, Zack and William turned to Ryan and Bridget and waved before turning a corner and heading down the corridor toward their gate.

Bridget wandered through the house for the next week in a daze. It was not due to a lack of options. In fact, all she had to do was look around the neighborhood for numerous ideas about how to spend her free time now that her children were gone. The vast majority of empty nesters seemed to kill time exercising. A day didn't pass without one of her mature neighbors exclaiming that they were in the best shape of their lives. But exercising held no appeal for Bridget. It seemed to her that no matter how buff your body, if you ended up in a line-up next to a twenty-year-old, you didn't stand a chance. And wasn't exercising the thing you did when you lacked imagination? Volunteering was an option and, of course, she ought to get back to the art. There was no reason to put it off now. Another idea was to get a dog—from strollers to leashes— every woman she knew attached herself first to one and then the other.

One day, a week after William's departure, Bridget finished her coffee and wandered upstairs to his room, where she sat for a long time staring at his log cabin wallpaper. They'd repapered the wall when he was ten. The night before

Christmas, they'd moved a sleeping William to their bed and spent the night constructing the bunk bed. Then they'd put him back in the lower bunk. When he woke up, he'd run down to the living room, and Bridget, seeing his radiant face, realized that nothing she'd ever bought for herself had given her half as much pleasure.

She lay down on the lower bunk, which had sagged into a crevasse under the weight of William's 180-pound, 5'10" frame. All these years, this had been the first thing he'd seen in the morning. On his bookshelf she thumbed through the chronicle of his reading life: Dr. Seuss, Arthur, *Harry Potter*, *The Chronicles of Narnia*, *Lord of the Rings*. Why had he kept his tenth grade AP US History book? Wasn't that the book he'd thrown against the wall in a fit of frustration?

Bridget took the AP US History book down from William's shelf and paged through it until she hit on the chapter on Jamestown and realized that although she'd heard the name a million times, she had absolutely no memory of what had taken place there. She sat down on the bed and began to read.

Sometime later, Bridget was awakened by the sound of a duck quacking. She opened her eyes. She was still on William's bed with the history book open beside her. She rolled over and extracted the iPhone from her pocket.

The text included a picture of William standing with his hand on a brick guardrail. Around him, crowds of mostly Asian people were bent at forty-five-degree angles trudging up a steep incline. William was standing in front of a watchtower. In several of the small openings in the turret, people were peeking through the apertures, smiling and waving down at the pedestrians below. In the background, the wall wound through a jumble of green hills before disappearing into the horizon. William stood in the middle of the photo, at the apex, giving the thumbs up.

"I made it!" his message read.

It was amazing to think that someone she'd given birth to was all the way on the other side of the world, wandering around, seeing the sights. Bridget pressed on the picture and zoomed in so that she could view everything around William: the hills, the sweat-soaked shirt of another man leaning against the wall, a group of three boys in navy shorts and white T-shirts running past. She scrolled over the towers and the cobblestones and stopped when she saw a young girl holding the hand of a woman who might have been her mother. They were standing about ten feet away from William. When Bridget looked closer, she could see that the little girl was crying and the mother was looking up at those last ten steps before the summit, probably thinking, *Why did I ever think this was a good idea?*

Bridget felt like a deity looking down on the whole scene from a great height. She wanted to reach down and pat the woman on the head.

ACKNOWLEDGMENTS

First, I would like to thank my husband, Fred, and my children: Jack, Charlie, Megan, and Peter Fordon, who are the best people I know.

I would also like to thank the writers who read and critiqued these stories: Whitney Bryant, Stephanie Early Green, Lolita Hernandez, Robin Martin, Linda Miller, Ellen Birkett Morris, Laura Hulthen Thomas, Joy Williams, and Alex Wilson.

Thanks also to Will Allison for editing these stories and providing much-needed encouragement, as well as the editors of the journals who first published them.

I'm so grateful for the Queens MFA program, as well as the Key West Literary Festival and the One Story Conference, where I kept on working and revising.

I cannot begin to express how indebted I am to the Jentel Artist Residency in Banner, Wyoming, for a month-long residency, which was such a productive period for me, and also reminded me that peace and quiet is pretty sweet.

A few notes:

Constellation Work (or Family Systems Constellations) is a revelatory form of therapy, and I really dig it, so I apologize to Bruce Hellinger for my skeptical protagonist. She had a lot to work through, and I'm sorry she took it out on you.

Apologies to my mother, who actually did write a cookbook called *How to Help Your Child Eat Right!* It may seem like I am taking a whack at the carrot people with the raisin eyes in this book, but I promise, Mom, they were delicious. Anyone would have preferred them to a Twinkie.

On a somber note, my neighborhood, like so many others, has seen a rise in both opioid overdoses and suicides. Please get help if you or someone you love needs it. The Substance Abuse and Mental Health Services Administration's (SAMHSA) National Helpline is 1-800-662-HELP (4357), and the National Suicide Prevention Hotline is 1-800-273-8255.

Last but not least, I am grateful to my publicist, Gregory Henry, as well as Jen Anderson, Jamie Jones, Annie Martin, Emily Nowak, Kristina Stonehill, Carrie Teefey, and everyone at Wayne State University Press. It has been a great honor working with you.

ABOUT THE AUTHOR

Kelly Fordon's work has appeared in *The Florida Review, The Kenyon Review (KRO), Rattle,* and various other journals. She is the author of three poetry chapbooks, including *On the Street Where We Live,* which won the 2012 Standing Rock Chapbook Award. Her most recent chapbook, *The Witness,* won the 2016 Eric Hoffer Award for the Chapbook and was shortlisted for the Grand Prize. Her short story collection, *Garden for the Blind,* was chosen as a Michigan Notable Book, a 2016 Foreword Reviews' INDIEFAB Finalist, a Midwest Book Award Finalist, an Eric Hoffer Finalist, and an IPPY Awards Bronze Medalist in the short story category. She teaches at the College for Creative Studies, Springfed Arts, and InsideOut Literary Arts Project in Detroit.